They must have been moving at 100 kph, and Bond knew he had almost lost control of the Bentley as it swerved across the road. He touched the brakes and felt the speed bleed off as the front wheels mounted the grass verge. There was a sliding sensation, then a rocking bump as they stopped. 'Get out!' Bond shouted. 'Out! On the far side! Use the car for cover!'

When he reached the relative safety of the car's side he saw Sukie had followed him, and was lying as though trying to push herself into the earth. Nannie, on the other hand, was crouched behind the boot, her cotton skirt hitched up to show a stocking top and part of a white suspender belt. The skirt had hooked itself on to a neat, soft leather holster, on the inside of her thigh, and she held a small .22 pistol in a two-handed grip, pointing across the boot.

'The law are going to be very angry,' Nannie shouted. 'They're coming back. Wrong side of the motorway.'

'What the hell . . .' Bond began.

'Get your gun and shoot at them,' Nannie laughed. 'Come on, Master James, Nannie knows best.'

By John Gardner

John Gardner served with the Fleet Air Arm and Royal Marines before embarking on a long career as a thriller writer, including international bestsellers *The Nostradamus Traitor*, *The Garden of Weapons*, *Confessor* and *Maestro*. In 1981 he was invited by Glidrose Publications Ltd – now known as Ian Fleming Publications – to revive James Bond in a brand new series of novels. To find out more visit John Gardner's website at www.john-gardner.com or the Ian Fleming website at www.ianfleming.com

NOBODY LIVES FOR EVER

John Gardner

For Peter and Peg
with affection

An Orion paperback

First published in Great Britain in 1986
by Jonathan Cape
This paperback edition published in 2012
by Orion Books Ltd,
Orion House, 5 Upper St Martin's Lane,
London WC2H 9EA

An Hachette UK company

1 3 5 7 9 10 8 6 4 2

A CIP catalogue record for this book
is available from the British Library.

ISBN 978-1-4091-3566-1

Typeset at The Spartan Press Ltd,
Lymington, Hants

Printed and bound by CPI Group (UK) Ltd,
Croydon, CR0 4YY

The Orion Publishing Group's policy is to use papers
that are natural, renewable and recyclable products and
made from wood grown in sustainable forests. The logging
and manufacturing processes are expected to conform to
environmental regulations of the country of origin.

www.orionbooks.co.uk
www.ianfleming.com

CONTENTS

I

THE ROAD SOUTH

James Bond signalled late, braked more violently than a Bentley driving instructor would have liked, and slewed the big car off the E5 motorway and on to the last exit road just north of Brussels. It was merely a precaution. If he was going to reach Strasbourg before midnight it would have made more sense to carry on, follow the ring road around Brussels, then keep going south on the Belgian N4. Yet even on holiday, Bond knew that it was only prudent to remain alert. The small detour across country would quickly establish whether anyone was on his tail, and he would pick up the E40 in about an hour or so.

Lately there had been a directive to all officers of the Secret Service, advising 'constant vigilance, even when off duty, and particularly when on leave and out of the country'.

He had taken the morning ferry to Ostend, and there had been over an hour's delay. About half-way into the crossing the ship had stopped, a boat had been lowered, and had moved out, searching the water in a wide circle. After some forty minutes the boat had returned and a helicopter appeared overhead as they set sail again. A little later the news spread throughout the ship. Two men overboard, and lost, it seemed.

'Couple of young passengers skylarking,' said the barman. 'Skylarked once too often. Probably cut to shreds by the screws.'

Once through Customs, Bond had pulled into a side street, opened the secret compartment in the dashboard of the Bentley Mulsanne Turbo, checked that his 9mm ASP automatic and the spare ammunition clips were intact, and taken out the small Concealable Operations Baton, which lay heavy in its soft leather holster. He had closed the compartment, loosened his belt and threaded the holster into place so that the baton hung at his right hip. It was an effective piece of hardware: a black rod, no more than fifteen centimetres long. Used by a trained man, it could be lethal.

Shifting in the driving seat now, Bond felt the hard metal dig comfortably into his hip. He slowed the car to a crawl of 40 kph, scanning the mirrors as he took corners and bends, automatically slowing again once on the far side. Within half an hour he was certain that he was not being followed.

Even with the directive in mind, he reflected that he was being more careful than usual. A sixth sense of danger or possibly M's remark a couple of days ago?

'You couldn't have chosen a more awkward time to be away, 007,' his chief had grumbled, though Bond had taken little notice. M was noted for a grudging attitude when it came to matters of leave.

'It's only my entitlement, sir. You agreed I could take my month now. If you remember, I had to postpone it earlier in the year.'

M grunted. 'Moneypenny's going to be away as well. Off gallivanting all over Europe. You're not . . . ?'

'Accompanying Miss Moneypenny? No, sir.'

'Off to Jamaica or one of your usual Caribbean haunts, I suppose,' M said with a frown.

'No, sir. Rome first. Then a few days on the Riviera dei Fiori before driving across to Austria – to pick up my housekeeper, May. I just hope she'll be fit enough to be brought back to London by then.'

'Yes . . . yes.' M was not appeased. 'Well, leave your full itinerary with the Chief-of-Staff. Never know when we're going to need you.'

'Already done, sir.'

'Take care, 007. Take special care. The Continent's a hotbed of villainy these days, and you can never be too careful.' There was a sharp, steely look in his eyes that made Bond wonder whether something was being hidden from him.

As Bond left M's office, the old man had the grace to say he hoped there would be good news about May.

At the moment, May, Bond's devoted old Scottish house-keeper, appeared to be the only worry on an otherwise cloudless horizon. During the winter she had suffered two severe attacks of bronchitis and seemed to be deteriorating. She had been with Bond longer than either cared to remember. In fact, apart from the Service, she was the one constant in his not uneventful life.

After the second bronchial attack, Bond had insisted on a thorough check-up by a Service-retained doctor with a Harley Street practice, and though May had resisted, insisting she was 'tough as an auld game bird, and no yet fit for the pot', Bond had taken her himself to the consulting rooms. There had followed an agonising week, with May being passed from specialist to specialist, complaining all the way. But the results of the tests were undeniable. The left lung was badly damaged, and there was a distinct possibility that the disease might spread. Unless the lung was removed immediately and the patient underwent at least three months of enforced rest and care, May was unlikely to see her next birthday.

The operation was carried out by the most skilful surgeon Bond's money could buy, and once she was well enough, May was packed off to a world-renowned clinic specialising in her complaint, the Klinik Mozart, in the mountains south of Salzburg. Bond telephoned the clinic regularly and was told that she was making astonishing progress.

He had even spoken to her personally the evening before, and he now smiled to himself at the tone of her voice, and the somewhat deprecating way she had spoken of the clinic. She was, no doubt, reorganising their staff and calling down the wrath of her Glen Orchy ancestors on everyone from maids to chefs.

'They dinna know how to cook a decent wee bite here, Mr James, that's the truth of it; and the maids canna make a bed for twopence. I'd no employ any the one of them – and you paying all this money for me to be here. Yon's a downright waste, Mr James. A *crinimal* waste.' May had never been able to get her tongue round the word 'criminal'.

'I'm sure they're looking after you very well, May.' She was too independent to be a really good patient.

Trust May, he thought. She liked things done her way or not at all. It would be purgatory for her in the Klinik Mozart.

He checked the fuel, deciding it would be wise to have the tank filled before the long drive that lay ahead on the E40. Having established that there was nobody on his tail, he concentrated on looking for a garage. It was after seven in the evening, and there was little traffic about. He drove through two small villages and saw the signs indicating proximity to the motorway. Then, on a straight, empty, stretch of road, he spotted the garish signs of a small filling station.

It appeared to be deserted and the two pumps unattended, though the door to the tiny office had been left open. A notice in red warned that the pumps were not self-service, so he pulled the Mulsanne up to the Super pump and switched off the engine. As he climbed out, stretching his muscles, he became aware of the commotion behind the little glass and brick building. Growling, angry, voices could be heard, and a thump, as though someone had collided with a car. Bond locked the car using the central locking device and strode quickly to the corner of the building.

Behind the office was a garage area. A white Alfa Romeo Sprint stood in front of the open doors. Two men were holding down a young woman on the bonnet. The driver's door was open and a handbag lay ripped open on the ground, its contents scattered.

'Come on,' one of the men said in rough French, 'where is it? You must have some! Give.' Like his companion, the thug was dressed in faded jeans, shirt and sneakers. Both were short, broad shouldered, with tanned muscular arms – rough customers by any standards. Their victim protested, and the man who had spoken raised his hand to hit her across the face.

'Stop that!' Bond's voice cracked like a whip as he moved forward.

The men looked up, startled. Then one of them smiled. 'Two for the price of one,' he said softly, grabbing the woman by the shoulder and throwing her away from the car.

The man facing Bond held a large wrench, and clearly thought Bond was easy prey. His hair was untidy, tight and curly, and the surly young face already showed the scars of an experienced street fighter. He leaped forward in a half crouch, holding the wrench low. He moved like a large monkey, Bond thought, as he reached for the baton on his right hip.

The baton, made by the same firm that developed the ASP 9mm pistol, looked harmless enough – fifteen centimetres of on-slip, rubber-coated metal. But, as he drew it from its holster, Bond flicked down hard with his right wrist. From the rubber-covered handle sprang a further, telescoped twenty-five centimetres of toughened steel, which locked into place.

The sudden appearance of the weapon took the young thug off guard. His right arm was raised, clutching the wrench, and for a second he hesitated. Bond stepped quickly to his left and swung the baton. There was an unpleasant cracking noise, followed by a yelp, as the baton connected with the attacker's forearm. He dropped the wrench and doubled up, holding his broken arm and cursing violently in French.

Again Bond moved, delivering a lighter tap this time, to the back of the neck. The mugger went on to his knees and pitched forward. With a roar, Bond hurled himself at the second thug. But the man had no stomach for a fight. He turned and started to run; not fast enough, though, for the tip of the baton came down hard on his left shoulder, certainly breaking bones.

He gave a louder cry than his partner, then raised his hands and began to plead. Bond was in no mood to be kind to a couple of young tearaways who had attacked a virtually helpless woman. He lunged forward, and buried the baton's tip into the man's groin, eliciting a further screech of pain which was cut off by a smart blow to the left of the neck, neatly judged to knock him unconscious but do little further damage.

Bond kicked the wrench out of the way, and turned to assist the young woman, but she was already gathering her things together by the car.

'You all right?' He walked towards her, taking in the Italianate looks – the long tangle of red hair, the tall, lithe body, oval face and large brown eyes.

'Yes. Thank you, yes.' There was no trace of accent. As he came closer, he noted the Gucci loafers, very long legs encased in tight Calvin Klein jeans, and a silk Hermes shirt. 'It's lucky you came along when you did. Do you think we should call the police?' She gave her head a little shake, stuck out her bottom lip and blew the hair out of her eyes.

'I just wanted petrol.' Bond looked at the Alfa Romeo. 'What happened?'

'I suppose you might say that I caught them with their fingers in the till, and they didn't take kindly to that. The attendant's out cold in the office.'

The muggers, posing as attendants, had apologised when she drove in, saying the pumps out front were not working. Could she take the car to the pump around the back? 'I fell for it, and they dragged me out of the car.'

Bond asked how she knew about the attendant?

'One of them asked the other if he'd be okay. He said the man would be out for an hour or so.' There was no sign of tension in her voice, and as she smoothed the jungle of hair, her hands were steady. 'If you want to be on your way, I can telephone the police. There's really no need for you to hang about, you know.'

'Nor you,' he said with a smile. 'Those two will also be asleep for some time. The name's Bond, by the way. James Bond.'

'Sukie.' She held out a hand, the palm dry and the grip firm. 'Sukie Tempesta.'

In the end, they both waited for the police, costing Bond over an hour and a half's delay. The pump attendant had been badly beaten and required urgent medical attention. Sukie did what she could for him while Bond telephoned the police. As they waited they talked and Bond tried to find out more about her, for the whole affair had begun to intrigue him. Somehow, he had the impression that she was holding out on him. But, however cleverly he phrased his questions, Sukie managed to sidestep with answers that told him nothing.

There was little to be gleaned from observation. She was very self-possessed, and could have been anything, from a lawyer to a society hostess. Judging by her appearance and the jewellery she wore, she was well off. Whatever her background, Bond decided that Sukie was certainly an attractive young woman, with a low-pitched voice, precise economic movements and a reserved manner that was possibly a little diffident.

One thing he did discover quickly was that she spoke at least three languages, which pointed to both intelligence and a good education. As for the rest, he could not even discover her nationality, though the plates on the Sprint were, like her name, Italian.

Before the police arrived in a flurry of sirens, Bond had returned to his car and stowed away the baton – an illegal weapon in any country. He submitted to an interrogation, and was asked to sign a statement. Only then was he allowed to fill up the car and leave, with the proviso that he gave his whereabouts for the next few weeks, and his address and telephone number in London.

Sukie Tempesta was still being questioned when he drove away, feeling strangely uneasy. He recalled the look in M's eyes; and began to wonder about the business on the ferry.

Just after midnight, he was on the E25 between Metz and Strasbourg. He had again filled the tank, and drunk some passable coffee at the French frontier. Now the road was almost deserted, so he spotted the tail lights of the car ahead a good four kilometres before overtaking it. He had set the cruise control at 110 kph after crossing the frontier, and so sailed past the big white BMW, which appeared to be pottering along in the fifties.

Out of habit, his eyes flicked to the car's plates and the number registered in his mind as did the international badge D, which identified the car as German.

A minute or so later, Bond became alert. The BMW had picked up speed, moving into the centre lane, yet remaining close to him. The distance varied between about five hundred to less than a hundred metres. He touched the brakes, switched back from cruise control and accelerated. One hundred and thirty. One hundred and forty! The BMW was still there.

Then, with about fifteen kilometres to go before the outskirts of Strasbourg, he became aware of another set of headlights directly behind him in the fast lane, and coming up at speed.

He moved into the middle lane, eyes flicking between the road ahead and the mirror. The BMW had fallen back a little, and in seconds the oncoming lights grew, and the Bentley was rocked slightly as a little black car went past like a jet. It must have been touching 160 kph and in his headlights Bond could get only a glimpse of the plates, which were splattered with mud. He thought they must be Swiss, as he was almost certain that he had caught sight of a Ticino Canton shield to the right of the rear plate. There was not enough time for him even to identify the make of the car.

The BMW remained in place for only a few more moments, slowing and losing ground. Then Bond saw the flash in his mirror: a brutal crimson ball erupting in the middle lane behind him. He felt the Bentley shudder under the shock waves and watched in the mirror as lumps of flaming metal danced across the highway.

Bond increased pressure on the accelerator. Nothing would make him stop and become involved at this time of night, particularly on a lonely stretch of road. Suddenly he realised that he felt oddly shaken at the unexplained violence which appeared to have surrounded him all day.

At one-eleven in the morning, the Bentley nosed its way into Strasbourg's Place Saint-Pierre-le-Jeune and came to a standstill outside the Hotel Sofitel. The night staff were deferential. Oui, M. Bond . . . Non, M. Bond. But certainly they had his reservation. The car was unloaded, his baggage whipped away, and he took the Bentley himself to the hotel's private parking.

The suite proved to be almost too large for the overnight stay, and there was a basket of fruit, with the compliments of the manager. Bond did not know whether to be impressed or on his guard. He had not stayed at the Sofitel for at least three years.

Opening the minibar, he mixed himself a martini. He was pleased the bar stocked Gordon's and a decent vodka, though he had to make do with a simple Lillet vermouth instead of his preferred Kina. Taking the drink over to the bed, Bond selected one of his two briefcases – the one that contained the sophisticated scrambling equipment. This he attached to the telephone and dialled Transworld Exports (the Service Headquarters' cover) in London.

The Duty Officer listened patiently while Bond recounted the two incidents in some detail. The line was quickly closed, and Bond, tired after the long drive, took a brief shower, rang down for a call at eight in the morning, and stretched out naked under the bedclothes.

Only then did he start to face up to the fact that he was more than a little concerned. He thought again of that strange look in M's eyes; then about the Ostend ferry and the two men overboard; the girl – Sukie – in distress at the filling station, and the appalling explosion on the road. There had been too many incidents to be mere coincidence, and a tiny suspicion of menace started to creep into his mind.

2

THE POISON DWARF

Bond sweated through his morning workout – the twenty slow pushups with their exquisite lingering strain; then the leg lifts, performed on the stomach; and lastly the twenty fast toe-touches.

Before going to the shower, he called room service and gave his precise order for breakfast: two thick slices of wholewheat bread, with the finest butter and, if possible, Tiptree Little Scarlet jam or Cooper's Oxford marmalade. Alas, Monsieur, there was no Cooper, but they had Tiptree. It was unlikely they could supply De Bry coffee, so after detailed questioning he settled for their special blend. While waiting for the tray to arrive, he took a very hot shower, followed by another with the water freezing cold.

A man of habit, Bond did not normally like change, but he had recently altered his soap, shampoo and cologne to Dunhill Blend 30, as he liked their specially masculine tang – and now, after a vigorous towelling, he rubbed the cologne into his body. Then he slipped into his silk travelling Happi-coat to await breakfast, which came accompanied by the local morning papers.

The BMW, or the débris that was left, seemed to be spread across all the front pages, while the headlines proclaimed the bombing to be everything from an atrocious act of urban terror-ism to the latest assassination in a criminal gang war that had been sweeping France over the last few weeks. There was little detail, except for the information given by the police, that there had been only one victim, the driver, and that the car had been registered in the name of Conrad Tempel, a German business-man from Freiburg. Herr Tempel was missing from his home, so they presumed he was among the fragments of the motor car.

While reading the story. Bond drank his two large cups of black coffee without sugar, and decided that he would skirt Freiburg later that day, after driving into Germany. He planned to cross the frontier again at Basle. Once in Switzerland, he would make his way down to Lake Maggiore in the Ticino Canton and spend a night in one of the small tourist villages on the Swiss side of the lake. Then he would make the final long run into Italy and the lengthy sweat down the autostradas to Rome. He would spend a few days with the Service's Resident and his wife, Steve and Tabitha Quinn.

Today's drive would be less taxing. He did not need to leave until noon, so he had a little time to relax and look around. But first there was the most important job of the day, the telephone call to the Klinik Mozart, to enquire after May.

He dialled 19, the French 'out' code, followed by the 61 which would take him into the Austrian system, then the number. Doktor Kirchtum came on the line almost immediately.

'Good morning, Mr Bond. You are in Belgium now, yes?'

Bond told him politely that he was in France, would be in Switzerland tomorrow, and in Italy the following day.

'You are burning a lot of the rubber, as they say.' Kirchtum was a small man, but his voice was loud and resonant. At the clinic he could be heard in a room long before he arrived. The nurses called him *das Nebelhorn*, the Foghorn.

Bond asked after May.

'She still does well. She orders us around, which is a good sign of recovery.' Kirchtum gave a guffaw of laughter. 'I think the chef is about to cash in his index, as I believe you English say.'

'Hand in his cards,' Bond said, smiling to himself. The Herr Doktor, he was sure, made very studied errors in colloquial

English. He asked if there was any chance of speaking to the patient, and was told that she was undergoing some treatment at the moment and would not be able to talk on the telephone until later in the day. Bond said he would try to telephone again during his drive through Switzerland, thanked the Herr Doktor, and was about to hang up when Kirchtum stopped him.

'There is someone here who would like a word with you, Mr Bond. Hold on. I'll put her through.'

To Bond's surprise, he heard the voice of M's PA, Miss Moneypenny, speaking to him with that hint of affection she always reserved for him.

'James! How lovely to talk to you.'

'Well, Moneypenny. What on earth are you doing at the Mozart?'

'I'm on holiday, like you, and spending a few days in Salzburg. I just thought I'd come up and see May. She's doing very well, James.' Moneypenny's voice sounded light and excited.

'Nice of you to think of her. Be careful what you get up to in Salzburg, though, Moneypenny – all those musical people looking at Mozart's house and going to concerts . . .'

'Nowadays all they want is to go and see the locations used in *The Sound of Music*,' she replied, laughing.

'Well, take care all the same, Penny. I'm told those tourists are after only one thing from a girl like you.'

'Would that you were a tourist, then, James.'

Miss Moneypenny still held a special place in her heart for Bond. After a little more conversation Bond again thanked her for the thoughtful action of visiting May.

His luggage was ready for collection, the windows were open and the sun streamed in. He would take a look around the hotel, check the car, have some more coffee and get on the road. As he went down to the foyer he realised how much he needed a holiday. It had been a hard, tough year, and for the first time Bond wondered if he had made the right decision. Perhaps the short trip to his beloved Royale-les-Eaux would have been a better idea.

A familiar face slid into the periphery of his vision as he crossed the foyer. Bond hesitated, turned and gazed absently into the hotel shop window, the better to examine the reflection of a man sitting near the main reception desk. He gave no sign of having seen Bond, as he sat casually glancing through yesterday's *Herald Tribune*. He was short, barely four feet two inches. Neatly and expensively dressed, he had the look of complete confidence characteristic of so many small men. Bond always mistrusted people of short stature, knowing their tendency to over-compensate with ruthless pushiness, as though it were necessary to prove themselves.

He turned away, having made his identification. The face was known well enough to him, with thin, ferret-like features and the same bright, darting eyes as the animal. What, he wondered to himself, was Paul Cordova – or the Rat as he was known in the underworld – doing in Strasbourg? Bond knew there had been a suggestion some years ago that the KGB, posing as a United States Government agency, had used him to do a particularly nasty piece of work in New York.

Paul, the Rat, Cordova was an enforcer – a polite term for a killer – for one of the New York Families, and his photograph and record were on the files of the world's major police and intelligence departments. It was part of Bond's job to know faces like this, even though Cordova moved in criminal rather than intelligence circles. But Bond did not think of him as the Rat. To him, the man was the Poison Dwarf. Was his presence in Strasbourg another 'coincidence'? Bond wondered.

He went down to the parking area, checked the Bentley carefully, and told the man on duty that he would be picking it up within half an hour. He refused to let any of the hotel staff move the car. Indeed, there had been a certain amount of surliness on his arrival because he would not leave the keys at the desk. On his way out, Bond could not fail to notice the low, black, wicked-looking Series 3 Porsche 911 Turbo. The rear plates were mud-spattered, but the Ticino Canton disc showed clearly. Whoever had raced past him on the motorway just before the destruction of the BMW was now at the hotel. Bond's antennae told him that it was time to get out of Strasbourg. The menacing small cloud had grown a shade larger.

Cordova was not in the hotel foyer when he returned. On reaching his room, Bond put through another call to Transworld Exports in London, again using the scrambler. Even on leave it was his duty to report on the movements of anyone like the Poison Dwarf, particularly so far away from his own patch.

Twenty minutes later, Bond was at the wheel of the Bentley, heading for the German border. He crossed without incident, skirted Freiburg, and by afternoon again crossed frontiers, at Basle. After a few hours' driving he boarded the car train for the journey through the St Gotthard Pass, and by early evening the Bentley was purring through the streets of Locarno and on to the lakeside road. Bond passed through Ascona, that paradise for artists, both professional and amateur, and on to the small and pleasing village of Brissago.

In spite of the sunlight and breathtaking views of clean Swiss villages, and towering mountains, a sense of impending doom remained with Bond as he travelled south. At first he put it down to the odd events of the previous day and the vaguely disconcerting experience of seeing a New York Mafia hood in Strasbourg. Yet, as he neared Lake Maggiore, he wondered if this mood could be due to a slightly dented pride. He felt distinctly annoyed that Sukie Tempesta had appeared so self-assured, calm and unimpressed by his charm. She could, he thought, at least have shown some sort of gratitude. Yet she had hardly smiled at him.

But when the red-brown roofs of the lakeside villages came in sight, Bond began to laugh. Suddenly his gloom lifted and he recognised his own pettiness. He slid a compact disc into the stereo player and a moment later the combination of the view and the great Art Tatum rattling out *The Shout* banished the darkness, putting him into a happier mood.

Though his favourite part of the country lay around Geneva, Bond also loved this corner of Switzerland that rubbed shoulders with Italy. As a young man he had lazed around the shores of Lake Maggiore, eaten some of the best meals of his life in Locarno, and once, on a hot moonlit night, with the waters off Brissago alive with lamp-lit fishing boats, in the very ordinary little hotel by the pier, had made unforgettable love to an Italian countess.

It was to this hotel, the Mirto du Lac, that he now drove. It was a simple family place, below the church with its arcade of cypresses, and near the pier where the lake steamers put in every hour. The *padrone* greeted him like an old friend, and Bond was soon ensconced in his room, with the little balcony looking down to the forecourt and landing stage.

Before unpacking Bond dialled the Klinik Mozart. The Herr Direktor was not available and one of the junior doctors told him politely that he could not speak to May because she was resting. There had been a visitor and she was a little tired. For some reason the words did not ring true. There was a slight hesitation in the doctor's voice which put Bond on the alert. He asked if May was all right, and the doctor assured him that she was perfectly well, just a little tired.

'This visitor,' he went on, 'I believe a Miss Moneypenny . . .'

'This is correct.' The doctor was the one who sounded most correct.

'I don't suppose you happen to know where she's staying in Salzburg?'

He did not. 'I understand she is coming back to see the patient tomorrow,' he added.

Bond thanked him and said he would call again. By the time he had showered and changed, it was starting to get dark. Across the lake the sunlight gradually left Mount Tamaro, and lights went on along the lakeside. Insects began to flock around the glass globes, and one or two couples took seats at the tables outside.

As Bond left his room to go down to the bar in the corner of the restaurant, a black Series 3 Porsche 911 crept quietly into the forecourt and parked with its nose thrust towards the lake. Its occupant climbed out, locked the car and walked with neat little steps back the way he had driven, up towards the church.

It was some ten minutes later that the people at the tables and in the hotel bar heard the repeated piercing screams. The steady murmur of conversation faded as it became obvious the screams were not part of some lighthearted game. These were shrieks of terror. Several people in the bar started towards the door. Some men outside were already on their feet, others were looking around to see where the noise was coming from. Bond was among those who hurried outside. The first thing he saw was the Porsche. Then a woman, her face white and her hair flying, her mouth stretched wide in a continuous scream, came running down the steps from the churchyard. Her hands kept going to her face, then wringing the air, then clutching her head. She was shouting, '*Assassinio! Assassinio!*' – Murder – as she pointed back to the churchyard.

Five or six men got up the steps ahead of Bond and clustered round a small bundle lying across the cobbled path, shocked into silence at the sight that confronted them.

Bond moved quietly to the perimeter of the group. Paul, the Rat, Cordova lay on his back, knees drawn up, one arm flung outwards, his head at an angle, almost severed by a single deep slash across the throat. Blood had already spread over the cobbles.

Bond pushed through the gathering crowd and returned to the lakeside. He had never believed in coincidences. He knew that the drownings, the affair at the filling station, the explosion on the motorway, and Cordova's appearance, here and in France, were linked, and that he was the common denominator.

His holiday was shattered. He would have to telephone London, report, and await orders.

Another surprise awaited him as he entered the hotel. Standing by the reception desk, looking as elegant as ever in a short blue-tinged leather outfit, probably by Merenlender, stood Sukie Tempesta.

3

SUKIE

'James Bond!' The delight seemed genuine enough, but with beautiful women you could never be sure.

'In the flesh,' he said as he moved closer. For the first time he really saw her eyes: large, brown with violet flecks, oval, and set off by naturally long, curling lashes. They were eyes, he thought, that could be the undoing or the making of a man. His own flicked down to the full, firm curve of her breasts under the well-fitting leather. She stuck out her lower lip, to blow hair from her forehead, as she had done the day before.

'I didn't expect to see you again.' Her wide mouth tilted in a warm smile. 'I'm so glad. I didn't get a chance to thank you properly yesterday.' She bobbed a mock curtsey. 'Mr Bond, I might even owe you my life. Thank you very much. I mean *very* much.'

He moved to one side of the reception desk so that he could watch her and at the same time keep an eye on the main doors. Instinctively, he felt danger close at hand. Danger by being close to Sukie Tempesta, perhaps.

Outside the commotion was still going on. There were police among the crowd and the sound of sirens floated down from the main street and the church above. Bond knew he needed his back against a wall all the time now. She asked him what was going on, and when he told her she shrugged.

'It's commonplace where I spend most of my time. In Rome,

murder is a fact of life nowadays, but somehow you don't expect it here in Switzerland.'

'It's commonplace anywhere.' Bond tried his most charming smile. 'But what are you doing here, Miss Tempesta – or is it Mrs, or even Signora?'

She wrinkled her nose prettily and raised her eyebrows. 'Principessa, actually – if we have to be formal.'

Bond lifted an eyebrow. 'Principessa Tempesta.' He dropped his head in a formal bow.

'Sukie,' she said with a wide smile, the large eyes innocent, yet with a tiny tinge of mockery. 'You must call me Sukie, Mr Bond. Please.'

'James.'

'James.' And at that moment the *padrone* came bustling up to complete her booking. As soon as he saw the title on the registration form everything changed to a hand-wringing, bowing comedy, causing Bond to smile wryly.

'You haven't yet told me what you're doing here,' he continued, over the hotel keeper's effusions.

'Could I do that over dinner? At least I owe you that.'

Her hand touched his forearm and he felt the natural exchange of static. Warning bells rang in his head. No chances, he thought, don't take chances with anybody, particularly anyone you find attractive.

'Dinner would be very pleasant,' he replied before once more asking what she was doing here on Lake Maggiore.

'My little motor car has broken down. There's something very wrong, according to the garage here – which probably means all they'll do is change the plugs. But they say it's going to take days.'

'And you're heading for?'

'Rome, naturally.' She blew at her hair again.

'What a happy coincidence.' Bond gave another bow. 'If I can be of service . . .'

She hesitated briefly. 'Oh, I'm sure you can. Shall we meet for dinner down here in half an hour?'

'I'll be waiting, Principessa.'

He thought he saw her nose wrinkle and her tongue poke out like a naughty schoolgirl as she turned to follow the *padrone* to her room.

In the privacy of his own room, Bond telephoned London again, to tell them about Cordova. He had the scrambler on, and as an afterthought asked them to run a check on both the Interpol computer and their own, on the Principessa Sukie Tempesta. He also asked the Duty Officer if they had any information about the BMW's owner, Herr Tempel of Freiburg. Nothing yet, he was told, but some material had been sent to M that afternoon.

'You'll hear soon enough if it's important. Have a nice holiday.'

Very droll, thought Bond as he packed away the scrambler, a CC500 which can be used on any telephone in the world and allows only the legitimate receiving party to hear the caller *en clair*. Each CC500 has to be individually programmed so that eavesdroppers can hear only indecipherable sounds, even if they tap in with a compatible system. It was now standard Service practice for all officers out of the country, on duty or leave, to carry a CC500, and the access codes were altered daily.

There were ten minutes to spare before he was due to meet Sukie, though Bond doubted she would be on time. He washed quickly, rubbing cologne hard into face and hair, and then put on a blue cotton jacket over his shirt. He went quickly downstairs and out to the car. There was still a great deal of police activity in the churchyard, and he could see that a crime team had set up lights where Cordova's body had been discovered.

Inside the car he waited for the courtesy lights to go out before he pressed the switch on the main panel, revealing the hidden compartment below. He checked the 9mm ASP and buckled its compact holster in place underneath his jacket, then secured the baton holster to his belt. Whatever was going on around him was dangerous. At least two lives had already been lost – probably more – and he did not intend to end up as the next cadaver.

To his surprise, Sukie was already at the bar when he got back into the hotel.

'Like a dutiful woman, I didn't order anything while I waited.'

'I prefer dutiful women.'

Bond slid on to the bar stool next to her, turning it slightly so that he had a clear view of anyone coming through the big glass doors at the front. 'What will you drink?'

'Oh no, tonight's on me. In honour of your saving *my* honour, James.'

Again her hand lightly brushed his arm, and he felt the same electricity. Bond capitulated.

'I know we're in Ticino, where they think grappa is good liquor. Still, I'll stick to the comic drinks. A Campari soda, if I may.'

She ordered the same, then the *padrone* bustled over with the menu. It was very *alla famiglia*, very *semplice*, he explained. It would make a change, Bond said, and Sukie asked him to order for them both. He said he would be difficult and change the menu around a little, starting with the *Melone con kirsch*, though he asked them to serve his without the kirsch. Bond disliked any food soused in alcohol.

'For the entree there's really only one dish, pasta excepted, in these parts, you'll agree?'

'The *coscia di agnello*?'

She smiled as he nodded. In the north these spiced chops were known as 'lamm-Gigot'. Here, among the Ticinese, they were less delicate in taste, but made delicious by the use of much garlic. Like Bond, Sukie refused any vegetables, but accepted the plain green salad which he also ordered, together with a bottle of Frecciarossa Bianco, the best white wine they appeared to supply. Bond had taken one look at the champagnes and pronounced them undrinkable, but 'probably reasonable for making a dressing', at which Sukie laughed. Her laugh was, Bond thought, the least attractive thing about her, a little harsh, maybe not entirely genuine.

When they were seated Bond wasted no time in offering to help her on her journey.

'I'm leaving for Rome in the morning. I'd be very pleased to give you a lift. That is, if the Principe won't be offended at a commoner bringing you home.'

She gave a little pout. 'He's in no position to be offended. Principe Pasquale Tempesta died last year.'

'I'm sorry, I . . .'

She gave a dismissive wave of the right hand. 'Oh, don't be sorry. He was eighty-three. We were married for two years. It was convenient, that's all.' She did not smile, or try to make light of it.

'A marriage of convenience?'

'No, it was just convenient. I like good things. He had money; he was old; he needed someone to keep him warm at night. In the Bible, didn't King David take a young girl – Abishag – to keep him warm?'

'I believe so. My upbringing was rather Calvinistic, but I do seem to recall the Lower Fourth sniggering over that story.'

'Well, that's what I was, Pasquale Tempesta's Abishag, and he enjoyed it. Now I enjoy what he left me.'

'For an Italian you speak excellent English.'

'I should. I *am* English. Sukie's short for Susan.' There was the smile again, and then the laugh, a little more mellow this time.

'You speak excellent Italian then.'

'And French, and German. I told you that yesterday, when you were trying to ask subtle questions, to find out about me.'

She reached forward, putting out a hand to cover his as it lay on the table beside his glass.

'Don't worry, James, I'm not a witch. But I can spot nosey questions. Comes from the nuns, then living with Pasquale's people.'

'Nuns?'

'I'm a good convent-educated girl, James. You know about girls who've been educated in convents?'

'A fair amount.'

She gave another little pout. 'I was pretty well brainwashed. Daddy was a broker – all very ordinary: home counties; mock Tudor house; two cars; one scandal. Daddy was caught out with some funny cheques and got five years in an open prison. Collapse of stout family. I'd just finished at the convent, and was all set to go to Oxford. That was out, so I answered an ad in *The Times* for a nanny, with a mound of privileges, to an Italian family of good birth: Pasquale's son, as it happened. It's an old title, like all the surviving Italian nobility, but with one difference. They still have property and money.'

The Tempestas had taken the new English nanny into the family as one of their own. The old man, the Principe, had become a second father to her. She became very fond of him, so when he proposed a marriage – which he described as *comodo* as opposed to *comodita* – Sukie saw a certain wisdom in taking up the offer. Yet even in that she showed shrewdness, careful to ensure that the marriage would in no way deprive Pasquale's two sons of their rightful inheritance.

'It did, to some extent, but they're both wealthy and successful in their own right, and they didn't object. You know old Italian families, James. Papa's happiness, Papa's rights, respect for Papa . . .'

Bond asked how the two sons had achieved success, and she hesitated for a fraction too long before going on airily.

'Oh, business. They own companies and that kind of thing – and, yes, James, I'll take you up on your offer of a ride to Rome. Thank you.'

They were half-way through the lamb when the *padrone* came hurrying forward, excused himself to Sukie, and bent to whisper that there was an urgent telephone call for Bond. He pointed towards the bar, where the telephone was off the hook.

'Bond,' he said quietly into the receiver.

'James, you somewhere private?' He recognised the voice immediately. It was Bill Tanner, M's Chief-of-Staff.

'No. I'm having dinner.'

'This is urgent. Very urgent. Could you . . . ?'

'Of course.' He put down the receiver and went back to the table to make his apologies to Sukie. 'It won't take long.' He told her about May being ill in the clinic. 'They want me to ring them back.'

In his room he set up the CC500 and called London. Bill Tanner came on the line straight away.

'Don't say anything, James, just listen. The instructions are from M. Do you accept that?'

'Of course.'

He had no alternative if Bill Tanner said he was speaking for the Chief of the Secret Service.

'You're to stay where you are and take great care.' There was anxiety in Tanner's voice.

'I'm due in Rome tomorrow, I . . .'

'Listen to me, James. Rome's coming to you. You, I repeat *you*, are in the gravest danger. Genuine danger. We can't get anyone to you quickly, so you'll have to watch your own back. But stay put. Understand?'

'I understand.' When Bill Tanner spoke of Rome coming to him, he meant Steve Quinn, the Service Resident in Rome. The same Steve Quinn Bond had planned to stay with for a couple of days. He asked why Rome was coming to him.

'To put you fully in the picture. Brief you. Try to get you out.' He heard Tanner take a quick breath at the other end of the line. 'I can't stress the danger strongly enough, old friend. The Chief suspected problems before you left, but we only got the hard intelligence in the last hour. M has flown to Geneva and Quinn is on his way there to be briefed. Then he will come straight to you. He'll be with you before lunch. In the meantime, trust nobody. For God's sake, just stay close.'

'I'm with the Tempesta girl now. Promised her a ride to Rome. What's the form on her?' Bond was crisp.

'We haven't got it all, but her connections seem clean enough. Certainly not involved with the Honoured Society. Treat her with care, though. Don't let her get behind you.'

'I was thinking of the opposite, as a matter of fact.' Bond's mouth moved into a hard smile, tinged with a hint of cruelty.

Tanner told him to keep her at the hotel. 'Stall her about Rome, but don't alert her. You really don't know who are your friends and who your enemies. Rome will give you the full strength tomorrow.'

'We won't be able to leave until late morning, I'm afraid,' he told Sukie, once back at the table. 'That was a business chum who's been to see my old housekeeper. He's passing through here tomorrow morning, and I really can't miss the chance of seeing him.'

She said it did not matter. 'I was hoping for a lie-in tomorrow anyway.' Could he detect an invitation in her voice?

They talked on and had coffee and a *fine* in the neat dining room, with its red and white checked tablecloths and gleaming cutlery, the two stolid north Italian waitresses attending the diners as though serving writs instead of food.

Sukie suggested they should sit at one of the tables outside the Mirto, but Bond made the excuse that it could be uncomfortable.

'Mosquitoes and midges tend to congregate around the lights. You'll end up with that lovely skin blotched. It's safer indoors.'

She asked what kind of business he was in, and he gave her the usual convincing if vague patter, which she appeared to accept. They talked of towns and cities they both enjoyed, and of food and drink.

'Perhaps I can take you to dinner in Rome,' Bond suggested. 'Without wanting to seem ungrateful, I think we can get something a little more interesting at Papa Giovanni's or the Augustea.'

'I'd love it. It's a change to talk to someone who knows Europe well. Pasquale's family are very Roman, I'm afraid. They don't really see much further than the Appian Way.'

Bond found it a pleasant evening, although he had to make some effort to appear relaxed after hearing the news from London. Now he had to get through the night.

They went up together, with Bond offering to escort Sukie to her room. They reached the door, and he had no doubts as to what should happen. She came into his arms easily enough, but when he kissed her she did not respond, but kept her lips closed tight, her body rigid. So, he thought, one of those. But he tried again, if only because he wanted to keep her in sight. This time she pulled away, gently putting her fingers to his mouth.

'I'm sorry, James. But no.' There was the ghost of a smile as she said, 'I'm a good convent girl, remember. But that's not the only reason. If you're serious, be patient. Now, goodnight, and thank you for the lovely evening.'

'I should thank *you*, Principessa,' he said with a touch of formality.

He watched as she closed her door, then went slowly to his own room, swallowed a couple of Dexedrine tablets and prepared to sit up all night.

4

THE HEAD HUNT

Steve Quinn was a big man, tall, broad, bearded and with an expansive personality, not the usual sort to get a responsible undercover position in the Service. They preferred what they called 'invisible men' – grey people who could vanish into a crowd. 'He's a big, bearded bastard,' Steve's wife, the petite blonde Tabitha, was often heard to remark.

Bond watched from behind his half-closed shutters as Quinn got out of a hired car and walked towards the hotel entrance. A few seconds later, the telephone rang and Mr Quarterman was announced. Bond told them to send him up.

Quinn was inside with the door locked almost before the knock had died in the air. He did not speak immediately, but went straight to the window and glanced down at the forecourt and the lake steamer which had just docked. The sheer beauty of the lake usually took the tourists' breath away when they disembarked, but this morning the loud yah-yahing of an English woman's voice could be heard, even in Bond's room, saying, 'I wonder what there is to see here, darling.'

Bond scowled, and Quinn gave a tiny smile, almost hidden by his beard. He looked at the remains of Bond's breakfast and mouthed noiselessly, asking if the place was clean.

'Spent the night going over it. Nothing in the telephone, or anywhere else.'

Quinn nodded. 'Okay.'

Bond asked why they could not have flown Geneva up to him.

'Because Geneva's got problems of his own,' said Quinn, his finger stabbing out towards Bond. 'But not a patch on your problems, my friend.'

'Talk, then. The Chief met you for a briefing?'

'Right. I've done what I can. Geneva doesn't like it, but two of my people should be here by now to watch your back. M wants you in London – in one piece if possible.'

'So, there is someone on my tail.' Bond sounded unconcerned, but pictures of the shattered car on the motorway and Cordova's body lying in the churchyard flashed through his mind.

Quinn lowered himself into a chair. He spoke in a near whisper.

'No,' he said, 'you haven't got some*one* on your tail. It seems to us that you've got just about every willing terrorist organisation, criminal gang and unfriendly foreign intelligence service right up your rectum. There's a contract out for you. A unique contract. Somebody has made an offer – to coin a phrase – none of them can refuse.'

Bond gave a hard, half-smile. 'Okay, break it to me gently. What am I worth?'

'Oh, they don't want all of you. Just your head.'

Steve Quinn filled in the rest of the story. M had received a hint about two weeks before Bond went on leave. 'The Firm that controls South London tried to spring Bernie Brazier from the Island,' he began. In other words, the most powerful underworld organisation in South London had tried to get one Bernie Brazier out of the high security prison at Parkhurst, on the Isle of Wight. Brazier was doing life for the cold-blooded killing of a notorious London underworld figure. Scotland Yard knew he had carried out at least twelve other murders, although they could not prove it. In short, Bernie Brazier was Britain's top mechanic, a polite name for hired killer.

'The escape was bungled. A real dog's breakfast. Then after it was all over, friend Brazier wanted to do a deal,' Quinn continued, 'and, as you know, the Met don't take kindly to deals. So he asked to see somebody from the sisters.'

He spoke of their sister organisation, MI5. This had been refused, but the details were passed to M, who sent their toughest interrogator to Parkhurst Prison. Brazier claimed he was being sprung to do a job that threatened the country's security. In return for giving them the goods, he wanted a new identity and a place in the sun, with money to singe if not actually to burn.

Bond remained oddly detached as Quinn described the nightmarish scene. He knew the devil incarnate in M would promise the world for hard intelligence, and that in the end he would give his source the minimum. So it had been. Two more interrogators had gone to Parkhurst and had a long talk with Brazier. Then M had taken the trip himself to make the deal.

'And Bernie told all?' he finally asked.

'Part of it. The rest was to come once he was nicely tucked away in some tropical paradise with enough birds and booze to give him a coronary within a year.' Quinn's face went very hard. 'The day after M's visit they found Bernie in his cell – hanged with piano wire.'

From outside came the sound of children playing near the jetty, the toot of one of the lake boats, and far away the drone of a light aeroplane. Bond asked what they had got from the late Bernie Brazier.

'That you were the target for this unique contract. A kind of competition.'

'Competition?'

'There are rules, it appears, and the winner is the group that brings your head to the organisers – on a silver charger, no less. Any bona fide criminal, terrorist, or intelligence agency can enter. They have to be accepted by the organisers. The starting date was four days ago, and there's a time limit of three months. The winner gets ten million Swiss.'

'Who in heaven's name . . . ?' Bond started.

'M discovered the answer to that less than twenty-four hours ago, with the help of the Metropolitan Police. About a week back, they pulled in half of the South London mob, and let M's heavy squad have a go. It paid off, or M's paying off, I don't quite know which. I do know that four major London gangland chiefs are pleading for round the clock protection, and I guess they need it. The fifth laughed at M and walked out of the slammer. I gather they found him last night. He was not in good health.'

When Quinn went into the details of the man's demise, even Bond felt queasy. 'Jesus . . .'

'. . . Saves.' Quinn showed not a shred of humour. 'One can but hope He's saved that poor bastard. Forensic say he took an unconscionable time a-dying.'

'And who's organised this grisly competition?'

'It's even got a name, by the way.' Quinn sounded offhand. 'It's called the Head Hunt. No consolation prizes, just the big one. M reckons that around thirty professional killers went through the starting gate.'

'Who's behind it?'

'Your old friends the Special Executive for Counter-intelligence, Terrorism, Revenge and Extortion – SPECTRE; in particular, the successor to the Blofeld dynasty, whom you've had one nasty brush with already, M tells me . . .'

'Tamil Rahani. The so-called Colonel Tamil Rahani.'

'Who will be the late Tamil Rahani in a matter of three to four months. Hence the time limit.'

Bond was silent for a minute. He was fully aware of how dangerous Tamil Rahani could be. They had never really discovered how he had managed to take over as Chief Executive of SPECTRE, which seemed always to have kept its leadership within the Blofeld family. But certainly the inventive, brilliant strategist, Tamil Rahani, had become SPECTRE's leader. Bond could see the man now – dark-skinned, muscular, radiating dynamism. He was a ruthless, internationally powerful leader.

He recalled the last time he had seen Rahani, drifting by parachute over Geneva. His great forte as a commander was that he always led from the front. He had tried to have Bond killed about a month after that last meeting. Since then there had been few sightings, but 007 could well believe this bizarre competition was the brainchild of the sinister Tamil Rahani.

'Are you implying the man's on his way out? Dying?'

'There was a sudden escape by parachute . . .' Quinn did not look him in the eyes.

'Yes.'

'I'm told that he jarred his spine on landing. This set off a cancer affecting the spinal cord. Apparently six specialists have seen him. There is no hope. Within four months, Tamil Rahani's going to be the late Tamil Rahani.'

'Who's involved, apart from SPECTRE?'

Quinn slid a hand down his dark beard, 'M's working on it. A lot of your old enemies, of course. For starters, whatever they call the former Department V of the KGB these days – what used to be SMERSH . . .'

'Department Eight of Directorate S: KGB,' Bond snapped.

Quinn went on as though he had not heard: '. . . Then practically every known terrorist organisation, from the old Red Brigade to the Puerto Rican FALN – the Armed Forces for National Liberation. With ten million Swiss francs as the star prize you've attracted a lot of attention.'

'You mentioned the underworld.'

'Of course – British, French, German, at least three Mafia families and, I fear, the Union Corse. Since the demise of your ally, Marc-Ange Draco, they've been less than helpful . . .'

'All right!' Bond stopped him sharply.

Steve Quinn lifted his large body from the chair. There was none of the visible effort that might be expected from a man of his size, just a fast movement, a second between his being seated and standing, with one large hand on Bond's shoulder. 'Yes.

Yes, I know, this is going to be a bitch.' He hesitated. 'There's one more thing you ought to know about Head Hunt . . .'

Bond shook off the hand. Quinn had been tactless in reminding him of the special relationship he had once nurtured between the Service and the Union Corse, an organisation that could be even more deadly than the Mafia. Bond's contacts with the Union Corse had led to his marriage, followed quickly by the death of his bride, Marc-Ange Draco's daughter.

'What other thing?' he snapped. 'You've made it plain I can't trust anybody. Can I even trust you?'

With a sense of disgust, Bond recognised the truth of the last remark. He could trust nobody, not even Steve Quinn, the Service's man in Rome.

'It's to do with SPECTRE's rules for Head Hunt.' Quinn's face was expressionless. 'The contenders are restricted to putting one man in the field – one only. The latest information is that already four have died violently, within the past twenty-four hours – one of them only a few hundred metres from where we're sitting.'

'Tempel, Cordova and a couple of thugs on the Ostend ferry.'

'Right. The ferry passengers were representatives from two London gangs – South London and the West End. Tempel had links with the Red Army Faction. He was an underworld-trained hood and a barroom politician trying for the rich pickings in the politics of terrorism. Paul Cordova you know about.'

All four, Bond thought, had been very close indeed when they were murdered. What were the odds on that being a coincidence? Aloud, he asked Quinn what M's orders were.

'You're to get back to London as quickly as you can. We haven't the manpower available to look after you loose on the Continent. My own people will see you to the nearest airport and then take care of the car . . .'

'No.' Bond spat the word. 'I'll get the car back. Nobody else is going to take care of it for me – right?'

Quinn shrugged. 'Your funeral. You're vulnerable in that car.'

Bond was already moving about the room finishing his packing, yet all the time his senses were centred on Quinn. Trust nobody: right, he would not even trust this man.

'Your boys?' he said. 'Give me a rundown.'

'They're out there. Look for yourself.' Quinn nodded in the direction of the window. He crossed to the long shutters and peered through the louvred slats. Bond placed himself just behind the big man.

'There,' said Quinn, 'the one standing by the rocks, in the blue shirt. The other's in the silver Renault parked at the end of the row of cars.'

It was a Renault 25 V6i, not Bond's favourite kind of car. If he played his cards properly he could outrun that pair with ease.

'I want information on one other person,' he said as he stepped back into the centre of the room, 'an English girl with an Italian title . . .'

'Tempesta?' There was a sneer on Quinn's lips.

Bond nodded.

'M doesn't think she's part of the game, though she could be bait. He says you should take care. His words were "Exercise caution." She's around, I gather.'

'Very much so. I've promised to give her a lift to Rome.'

'Dump her!'

'We'll see. Okay, Quinn, if that's all you have for me, I'll sort out my route home. It could be scenic.'

Quinn nodded and stuck out his hand, which Bond ignored. 'Good luck. You're going to need it.'

'I don't altogether believe in luck. Ultimately I believe in only one thing – myself.'

Quinn frowned, nodded and left Bond to make his final preparations. Speed was essential, but his main concern at this moment was what he should do about Sukie Tempesta. She was there, an unknown quantity, yet he felt she could be used somehow. As a hostage, perhaps? The Principessa Tempesta would make an adequate hostage, a shield even, if he felt sufficiently ruthless. As though by telepathy, the telephone rang and Sukie's mellow voice came on the line.

'I was wondering what time you wanted to leave, James?'

'Whenever it suits you. I'm almost ready.'

She laughed, and the harshness seemed to have gone. 'I've nearly finished packing. I'll be fifteen minutes at the most. Do you want to eat here before we leave?'

Bond said he'd prefer to stop somewhere on the way, if she did not mind. 'Look, Sukie, I've got a small problem. It might involve a slight detour. May I come and talk to you before we go?'

'In my room?'

'It would be better.'

'It could also cause a small scandal for a well brought up convent girl.'

'I can promise you there'll be no scandal. Shall we say ten minutes time?'

'If you insist.' She was not being unpleasant, just a little more formal than before.

'It is rather important. I'll be with you in ten minutes.'

Hardly had he put down the telephone and snapped the locks on his case, when it rang again.

'Mr Bond?' He recognised the booming voice of Doktor Kirchtum, Direktor of the Klinik Mozart. He seemed to have lost some of his ebullience.

'Herr Direktor?' Bond heard the note of anxiety in his own tone.

'I'm sorry, Mr Bond. It is not good news . . .'

'May!'

'Your patient, Mr Bond. She is vanished. The police are here with me now. I'm sorry not to have made contact sooner. But she is vanished with the friend who visited yesterday, the Moneypenny lady. There has been a telephone call and the police wish to speak to you. She has been, how do you say it? Napped . . .'

'Kidnapped? May kidnapped, and Moneypenny?'

A thousand thoughts went through his head, but only one made sense. Someone had done his homework very well. May's kidnapping could just possibly have been associated with Moneypenny's, who was always a prime target. What was more probable, however, was that one of the Head Hunt contenders wanted Bond under close observation, and how better than to lead him in a search for May and Moneypenny?

5

NANNIE

All things considered, Bond thought, Sukie Tempesta showed that she was an uncommonly cool lady. He dropped the Happi-coat on to the bed, ready to pack later, and caught sight of his naked body in the long mirror. What he saw pleased him, not in any vain way, but because of his obvious fitness: the taut muscles of his thighs and calves, and the bulge of his biceps.

He had showered and shaved before Quinn's arrival, and now he dressed as he worked out a viable plan to deal with Sukie. He put on casual slacks, his favourite soft leather moccasins and a Sea Island cotton shirt. To hide the 9mm ASP, he threw on a battledress-style grey Oscar Jacobson Alcantara jacket. He placed his case and the two briefcases near the door, checked the gun, and went quickly downstairs, where he settled both his own and Sukie's accounts. He then went straight up to her room.

Sukie's Gucci luggage stood in a neat line near the door, which she opened to his knock. She was back in the Calvin Klein jeans, this time with a black silk shirt which looked to Bond like Christian Dior.

Gently he pushed her back into the room. She did not protest, but said simply that she was ready to leave. Bond's face was set in a serious mask, which made her ask, 'James, what is it? Something's really wrong, isn't it?'

'I'm sorry, Sukie. Yes. Very serious for me, and it could be dangerous for you too.'

'I don't understand . . .'

'I have to do certain things you might not like. You see, I've been threatened . . .'

'Threatened? How threatened?' She continued to back away.

'I can't go into details now, but it's clear to me – and others – that there's a possibility you could be involved.'

'Me? Involved with what, James? Threatening you?'

'It *is* a serious business, Sukie. My life's at risk, and we met in rather dubious circumstances . . .'

'Oh? What was dubious about it? Except for those unpleasant young muggers?'

'It seemed as though I came along at a fortunate moment, and that I saved you from some unpleasantness. Then your car breaks down, conveniently near where I'm staying. I offer you a lift to Rome. Some might see it as a set-up, with me as the target.'

'But I don't . . .'

'I'm sorry, I . . .'

'You can't take me to Rome?' Her voice was level. 'I understand, James. Don't worry about it, I'll find some way, but it does present me with a little problem of my own . . .'

'Oh, you're coming with me, maybe even to Rome eventually. I have no alternative. I have to take you, even if it's as a hostage. I must have a little insurance with me. You'll be my policy.'

He paused, letting it sink in, then, to his surprise, she smiled and said, 'Well, I've never been a hostage before. It'll be a new experience.'

She looked down and saw the gun in his hand.

'Oh, James! Melodrama? You don't need that. I'm on a kind of holiday anyway. I really don't mind being your hostage, if it's necessary.' She paused, her face registering a fascinated pleasure. 'It could even be exciting, and I'm all for excitement.'

'The kind of people I'm up against are about as exciting as tarantulas, and lethal as sidewinders. I hope what's going to happen now isn't going to be too nasty for you, Sukie, but I have no other option. I promise you this is no game. You're to do everything I say, and do it very slowly. I'm afraid I have to ask you to turn around – right around – with your hands on your head.'

He was looking for both a makeshift weapon and one more cunningly concealed. Sukie wore a small cameo brooch at the neck of her shirt. He made her unpin the brooch and throw it gently on to the bed, where her shoulder bag lay. Then he told her to take off her shoes.

He kept the cameo; it looked safe, but he knew technicians could do nasty things with brooch pins. He performed the entire examination deftly with one hand, while he held the ASP well back in the other. The shoes were clean, as was her belt. He apologised for the indignity, but her clothes, and person, were the first priorities. If she carried nothing suspicious he could deal with the luggage later, making sure it was kept out of harm's way until they stopped somewhere. He emptied the shoulder bag on to the bed. The usual feminine paraphernalia spilled out over the white duvet – including a cheque book, diary, credit cards, cash, tissues, comb, a small bottle of pills, crumpled Amex and Visa receipts, a small Cacharel Anaïs Anaïs spray, lipstick and a gold compact.

He kept the comb, some book matches, a small sewing kit from the Plaza Athénée, the scent spray, lipstick and compact. The comb, book matches and sewing kit were immediately adaptable weapons for close-quarter work. The spray, lipstick and compact needed further inspection. In his time Bond had known scent sprays to contain liquids more deadly than even the most repellent scent, lipsticks to house razor-sharp curved blades, propellants of one kind or another, even hypodermic syringes, and powder compacts that were miniature radios, or worse.

Sukie was more embarrassed than angry about having to strip. Her body was the colour of rich creamed coffee, smooth and regular, the kind of tan you can get only through patience, the right lotions, a correct regimen of sun, and nudity. It was the sort of body that men dreamed of finding alive and wriggling in their beds.

Bond went through the jeans and shirt, making sure there was nothing inserted into linings or stitching. When he was satisfied, he apologised again, told her to get dressed and then call the concierge. She was to use his exact words, saying that the luggage was ready in her room and in Mr Bond's. It was to be taken straight to Mr Bond's car.

Sukie did as she was told. As she put down the receiver, she gave a little shake of the head. 'I'll do exactly what you tell me, James. You're obviously desperate, and you're also undoubtedly a professional of some kind. I'm not a fool. I like you. I'll do anything, within reason, but I too have a problem.' Her voice shook slightly, as though the whole experience had unnerved her.

Bond nodded, indicating that she should tell him her problem.

'I've an old school friend in Cannobio, just along the coast . . .'

'Yes, I know Cannobio, a one-horse Italian holiday resort. Picturesque in a touristy kind of way. Not far.'

'I'm afraid I told her we'd pick her up on our way through. I was meant to meet her last night. She's waiting at that rather lovely church on the lakeside – the Madonna della Pietà. She'll be there from noon onwards.'

'Can we put her off? Telephone her?'

Sukie shook her head. 'After I arrived with the car problems, I telephoned the hotel where she was supposed to be staying. That was last night. She hadn't arrived. I called her again after dinner, and she was waiting there. They were fully booked. She was going in search of somewhere else. You'd said we might be late setting off so I just told her to be at the Madonna della Pietà from twelve noon. I didn't think of getting her to call back . . .'

She was interrupted by the *padrone* himself, arriving to collect the luggage.

Bond thanked him, said they would be down in a few minutes, and turned his mind to the problem. There was a big distance to cover, whatever he did. His aim was to get to the Klinik Mozart,

where there would be a certain amount of police protection
because of the search for May and Moneypenny. He had no wish
to go into Italy at all, and from what he could recall of the centre
of Cannobio, it was the perfect place for a set-up. The lakeside
road and the front of the Madonna della Pietà were always busy,
for Cannobio was a thriving industrial centre as well as holiday-
makers' paradise. The square in front of the church was ideal
territory for one man, or a motorcycle team, to make a kill. Was
Sukie, knowingly or not, putting him on the spot?

'What's her name, this old school friend?' he asked, sharply.

'Norrich.' She spelled it out for him. 'Nannette Norrich. Everyone calls her Nannie. Norrich Petrochemicals, that's Daddy.'

Bond nodded. He had already guessed. 'We'll pick her up but
she'll have to go along with my plans.' He took her firmly by the
elbow, to let her know he was in charge.

Bond knew that the trip to Cannobio would hold him up for
only an hour, thirty minutes there, and another thirty back,
before he could head off towards the frontier, and Austria. If he
took the risk, it would mean two hostages rather than one, and
he could position them in the car to make a hit more difficult.
There was also comfort in the thought that it was only his head
that would gain the prize. Whoever struck would have to do it
on a lonely stretch of road, or during a night stop. It was easy
enough to sever a human head. You did not even have to be very
strong. A flexi-saw – like a bladed garrotte – would do it in no
time. What would be essential to accomplish the task was a
certain amount of privacy. Nobody would have a go in front of
the main church in Cannobio, beside Lake Maggiore.

Outside, the *padrone* stood, at the rear of the British racing
green Mulsanne Turbo, waiting patiently with the luggage. From
the corner of his eye, Bond spotted Steve Quinn's man, who had
been standing above the rocks, begin to saunter casually back
along the cars towards the Renault. He did not even look in
Bond's direction, but kept his head down, as though searching

for something on the ground. He was tall, with the face of a Greek statue that had been exposed to much time and weather.

Bond contrived to keep Sukie between himself and the car, reaching forward from behind her to unlock the boot. When the luggage was stowed, they shook hands with the *padrone* with due solemnity, and Bond escorted Sukie to the front passenger side.

'I want you to fasten the seatbelt, then keep your hands in sight on the dashboard,' he said with a smile.

At the end of the line of cars the Renault's engine started up. Bond settled in the driving seat of the Bentley.

'Sukie, please don't do anything stupid. I promise that I can act much faster than you. Don't make me do anything I might regret.'

She smiled coyly. 'I'm the hostage. I know my place. Don't worry.'

They backed out, headed up the ramp and seven minutes later crossed the Italian frontier without incident.

'If you haven't noticed, there's a car behind us.' Sukie's voice wavered slightly.

'That's right.' Bond smiled grimly. 'They're babysitting us, but I don't want that kind of protection. We'll throw them off eventually.'

She nodded.

He had told her that Nannie would have to be handled carefully. She should not be told anything except that she could go on to Rome under her own steam. Plans had changed and they had to get to Salzburg in a hurry. 'Leave it to her. Let her make up her own mind. Be apologetic, but try to put her off. Follow me?'

There was a lot of activity going on around the Madonna della Pietà when they arrived. Standing by a small suitcase, looking supremely elegant, was a very tall young woman with hair the colour of a moonless night, pulled back into a severe bun. She wore a patterned cotton dress which the breeze caught for a second, blowing it against her body to reveal the outline of long, slim thighs, rounded belly and well-proportioned hips. She grinned as Sukie called her over to the passenger side of the car. 'Oh, how super! A Bentley. I adore Bentleys.'

'Nannie, meet James. We have a problem.'

She explained the situation, just as Bond had instructed her. All the time, he watched Nannie's calm face – the rather thin features, the dark grey eyes peering out brightly, through granny glasses, full of intelligence. Her eyebrows were unfashionably plucked, giving the attractive features a look of almost permanent sweet expectation.

'Well, I'm easy,' Nannie said in a low-pitched drawl, giving the impression that she did not believe a word of Sukie's tale. 'It's a holiday after all – Rome or Salzburg, it matters not. Anyway, I adore Mozart.'

Bond felt vulnerable out in the open, and could not allow the chattering to continue long. His tone implied urgency.

'Are you coming with us, Nannie?'

'Of course. I wouldn't miss it for the world.' Nannie had the door open, but Bond stopped her.

'Luggage in the boot,' he said a little sharply, then very quietly to Sukie, 'Hands in sight, like before. This is too important for games.'

She nodded and placed her hands above the dashboard, as Bond got out and watched Nannie Norrich put her case into the boot.

'Shoulder bag as well, please.' He smiled his most charming smile.

'I'll need it on the road. Why . . .'

'Please, Nannie, be a good girl. The problems Sukie told you about are serious. I can't have any luggage in the car. When the time comes, I'll check your bag and let you have it back. Okay?'

She gave a curious little worried turn of the head, but did as she was told. The Renault, Bond noticed, was parked ahead of them, engine idling. Good, they thought he planned to go on through Italy.

'Nannie, we've only just met and I don't want you to get any ideas, but I have to be slightly indelicate,' he said quietly. There were a lot of people around, but what he had to do was unavoid-able. 'Don't struggle or yell at me. I have to touch you, but I promise you, I'm not taking liberties.'

He ran his hands expertly over her body, using his fingertips and trying not to make it embarrassing for her. He talked as he went through the quick frisk. 'I don't know you, but my life's at risk, so if you get into the car you're also in danger. As a stranger you could also be dangerous to me. Do you understand?'

To his surprise, she smiled at him. 'Actually, I found that rather pleasant. I don't understand, but I still liked it. We should do it again sometime. In private.'

They settled back in the car and he asked Nannie to fasten her seat belt as there would be fast driving ahead. He started the engine again and waited for the right amount of space in the traffic. Then he put the Bentley into reverse, spun the wheel, banged at the accelerator and brake, and slewed the car back-wards into a skid, bringing the rear around in a half circle. He roared off, cutting in between a creeping Volkswagen and a truck load of vegetables – much to the wrath of the drivers.

Through the mirror he could see that the Renault had been taken by surprise. He increased speed as soon as the Bentley was through the restricted zone, and began to take the bends and winds of the lakeside road at a dangerous speed.

At the frontier he told the guards that he thought they were being followed by brigands, making much of his diplomatic passport, which he always carried for emergencies. The *carabin-ieri* were suitably impressed, called him *Eccellenza*, bowed to the ladies, and promised to question the occupants of the Renault with vigour.

'Do you always drive like that?' Nannie asked from the rear. 'I suppose you do. You strike me as a fast cars, horses and women kind of fellow. Action man.'

Bond did not comment. Violent man, he thought, con-centrating on the driving and leaving Sukie and Nannie to slip into talk of schooldays, parties and men.

There were some difficulties on the journey, particularly when his passengers wanted to use women's rooms. Twice during the afternoon they stopped at service areas, and Bond positioned the car so that he had a full view of the pay telephones and the women's room doors. He let them go one at a time, making pleasantly veiled threats as to what would happen to the one left in the car should the other do anything foolish. His own bladder had to be kept under control. Just before starting the long mountainous drive into Austria, they stopped at a roadside café and had some food. It was here that Bond took the chance of leaving the other two alone.

When he returned they both looked entirely innocent and even seemed surprised when he took a couple of benzedrine tablets with his coffee.

'We were wondering . . .' Nannie began.

'Yes?'

'We were wondering what the sleeping arrangements are going to be when we stop for the night. I mean, you obviously can't let us out of your sight . . .'

'You sleep in the car. I drive. There'll be no stopping at hotels. This is a one-hop run . . .'

'Very Chinese,' Sukie muttered.

'. . . and the sooner we get to Salzburg, the sooner I can release you. The local police will take charge of things after that.'

Nannie spoke up, level-voiced, the tone almost one of admonition. 'Look, James, we hardly know one another, but you have to understand that, for us, this is a kind of exciting adventure – something we only read about in books. It's obvious that you're on the side of the angels, unless our intuition's gone seriously wrong. Can't you confide in us just a little? We might be more help to you if we knew some more . . .'

'We'd better get back to the car,' Bond said flatly. 'I've already explained to Sukie that it's about as exciting as being attacked by a swarm of killer bees.'

He knew that Sukie and Nannie were either going through a

transition, starting to identify with their captor, or were trying to establish a rapport in order to lull him into complacency. To increase his chances of survival he had to remain detached, and that was not easy with two young women as attractive and desirable as they were.

Nannie gave a sigh of exasperation, and Sukie started to say something, but Bond stopped her with a movement of his hand.

'Into the car,' he ordered.

They made good time on the long drag up the twisting Malojapass and through St Moritz, finally crossing into Austria at Vinadi. Just before seven-thirty, having skirted Innsbruck, they were cruising north-east along the A12 autobahn. Within the hour they would turn east on the A8 to Salzburg. Bond drove with relentless concentration, cursing his situation. So beautiful was the day, so impressive the ever-changing landscape that, had things been different, this could have been a memorable holiday indeed. He searched the road ahead, scanning the traffic, then swiftly checked his speed, fuel consumption and the temperature of the engine.

'Remember the silver Renault, James?' said Nannie in an almost teasing voice from the rear. 'Well, I think it's coming up behind us fast.'

'Guardian angels,' Bond breathed. 'The devil take guardian angels.'

'The plates are the same,' Sukie said. 'I remember them from Brissago, but I think the occupants have changed.'

Bond glanced in the mirror. Sure enough, a silver Renault 25 was about eight hundred metres behind them. He could not make out the passengers. He remained calm; after all, they were only Steve Quinn's people. He pulled into the far lane, watching from his offside wing mirror.

He was conscious of a tension in the two girls, like game that has sensed the hunter. Fear suddenly seemed to flood the interior of the car, almost tangibly.

The road ahead was an empty, straight ribbon, with grassland curving upwards on either side to outcrops of rock and pine and fir forests. Bond's eyes flicked to the wing mirror again, and he saw the concentration on the face of the Renault's driver.

The low red disc of the sun was behind them. Perhaps the silver car was using the old fighter pilot tactic – out of the sun . . . As the Bentley swung for a second, the crimson fire filled the wing mirror. The next moment. Bond was pressing down on the accelerator, feeling the proximity of death.

The Bentley responded as only that machine can, with a surge of power effortlessly pushing them forward. But he was a fraction late. The Renault was almost abreast of them and going flat out.

He heard one of the women shout and felt a blast of air as a rear window was opened. He drew the ASP and dropped it in his lap, then reached towards the switches that operated the electric windows. Somehow he realised that Sukie had shouted for them to get down, while Nannie Norrich had lowered her window with the individual switch.

'On to the floor!'

He heard his own voice as his window slid down to the pressure of his thumb on the switch and a second blast of air began to circulate within the car. Nannie was yelling from the rear, 'They're going to shoot', and the distinctive barrel of a pump-action sawn-off Winchester showed for a split second from the rear window of the Renault.

Then came the two blasts, one sharp and from behind his right shoulder, filling the car with a film of grey mist bearing the unmistakable smell of cordite. The other was louder, but farther away, almost drowned by the engine noise, the rush of wind into the car and the ringing in his own ears.

The Mulsanne Turbo bucked to the right as though some giant metal boot-tip had struck the rear with force; at the same time there was a rending clattering noise, like stones hitting them. Then another bang came from behind him.

He saw the silver car to their left, almost abreast of them, a haze of smoke being whipped from the rear where someone crouched at the window, with the Winchester trained on the Bentley.

'Down, Sukie!' Bond yelled. It was like shouting at a dog, he thought, his voice rising to a scream as his right hand came up to fire through the open window. He aimed two rounds accurately at the driver.

There was a lurching sensation and a grinding as the sides of the two cars grated together, then drifted apart again, followed by another crack from the rear of the car.

They must have been moving at 100 kph, and Bond knew he had almost lost control of the Bentley as it swerved across the road. He touched the brakes and felt the speed bleed off as the front wheels mounted the grass verge. There was a sliding sensation, then a rocking bump as they stopped. 'Get out!' Bond shouted. 'Out! On the far side! Use the car for cover!'

When he reached the relative safety of the car's side he saw Sukie had followed him, and was lying as though trying to push herself into the earth. Nannie, on the other hand, was crouched behind the boot, her cotton skirt hitched up to show a stocking top and part of a white suspender belt. The skirt had hooked itself on to a neat, soft leather holster, on the inside of her thigh, and she held a small .22 pistol in a two-handed grip, pointing across the boot.

'The law are going to be very angry,' Nannie shouted. 'They're coming back. Wrong side of the motorway.'

'What the hell . . .' Bond began.

'Get your gun and shoot at them,' Nannie laughed. 'Come on, Master James, Nannie knows best.'

6

THE NUB

Over the long snout of the Bentley, Bond saw the silver Renault streaking back towards them, moving up the slow lane in the wrong direction, causing two other cars and a lorry to career across the wide autobahn to avoid collision. He had no time to go into the whys and wherefores of how he had missed finding Nannie's gun.

'The tyres,' she said coolly. 'Go for the tyres.'

'*You* go for the tyres,' Bond snapped, angry at being given instructions by this woman. He had his own method of stopping the car, which was now almost on top of them.

In the fraction before he fired, a host of thoughts crossed his mind. The Renault had originally contained a two-man team. When it reappeared there were three of them: one in the back with the Winchester, the driver and a back-up who seemed to be using a high-powered revolver. Somehow the man in the back had disappeared and the one in the passenger seat now had the Winchester. The driver's side window was open and in a fanatical act of lunacy, the passenger seemed to be leaning across the driver to fire the Winchester as they came up to the Mulsanne Turbo, which was slewed like a beached whale just off the hard shoulder of the road.

Bond was using the Guttersnipe sighting on the ASP, the three long bright grooves that gave the marksman perfect aim by showing a triangle of yellow when on target. He was on target now, not aiming at the tyres, but at the petrol tank. The ASP was loaded with Glaser Slugs, prefragmented bullets, containing No. 12 shot suspended in liquid Teflon. The impact from just one of these was devastating. It could penetrate skin, bone, tissue or metal before the mass of tiny steel balls exploded inside their target. The Slugs could cut a man in half at a few paces, remove a leg or arm, and certainly ignite a petrol tank.

Bond began to take up the first pressure on the trigger. As the rear of the Renault came fully into his sights, he squeezed hard and got the two shots away. He was conscious of the double crack from his left. Nannie was giving the tyres hell. Then several things happened quickly. The nearside front tyre disintegrated in a terrible burning and shredding of rubber. Bond remembered thinking that Nannie had been very lucky to get a couple of puny .22 shots so close to the inner section of the tyre.

The car began to slew inwards, toppling slightly as though it would cartwheel straight into the Bentley, but the driver struggled with wheel and brakes and the silver car just about stayed in line, running fast and straight towards the hard shoulder, hopelessly doomed. At the same time as the tyre disintegrated, the two Glaser Slugs from the ASP scorched through the bodywork and into the petrol tank.

Almost in slow motion, the Renault seemed to continue on its squealing, unsteady course. Then, just as it passed the rear of the Bentley, a long, thin sheet of flame, like natural gas being burned off hissed from the back of the car. There was even time to notice that the flame was tinged with blue before the whole rear end of the Renault became a rumbling, irregular, growing crimson ball.

The car began to cartwheel, a burning, twisted wreck, about a hundred metres beyond the Bentley, before the noise reached them: a great hiss and whump, followed by a screaming of rubber and metal as it went through its spectacular death throes.

Nobody moved for a second, then Bond reacted. Two or three cars were approaching the scene, and he was in no mood to be involved with the police at this stage.

'What kind of shape are we in?' he called.

'Dented, and there are a lot of holes in the bodywork, but the wheels seem okay. There's a very nasty scrape down this side. Stem to stern.'

Nannie was the other side of the car. She unhitched her skirt from the suspender belt, showing a fragment of white lace as she did so. Bond asked Sukie if she was okay.

'Shaken, but undamaged, I think.'

'Get in, both of you,' said Bond crisply. He dived towards the driving seat, conscious of at least one car containing people in checked shirts and sun hats cautiously drawing up near the burning wreckage. He twisted the key almost viciously in the ignition and the huge engine throbbed into life. He knocked off the main brake with his left hand, slid into drive and smoothly took the Mulsanne back on to the autobahn.

The traffic was still light, giving Bond the opportunity to check the car's engine and handling. There was no loss of fuel, oil or hydraulic pressure; he went steadily up through the gears and back again. The brakes appeared unaffected. The cruise control went in and came out normally, and the damage to the coachwork did not seem to have affected either the suspension or handling.

After five minutes he was satisfied that the car was relatively undamaged, though he did not doubt there was a good deal of penetration to the bodywork from the Winchester blasts. The Bentley would now be a sitting target for the Austrian police, who were unlikely to be enamoured of shoot-outs between cars on their relatively safe autobahns – particularly when the participants ended up incinerated. He needed to reach a telephone quickly and alert London, to get them to call the Austrian police off. Bond was also concerned about the fate of Quinn's team. Or could that have been his team, turned rogue hunters for the Swiss millions? Another image nagged at his mind – Nannie Norrich with the lush thigh exposed and the expertly handled .22 pistol.

'I think you'd better let me have the armoury, Nannie,' he said quietly, hardly turning his head.

'Oh, no, James. No, James. No, James, no,' she sang, quite prettily.

'I don't like women roving around with guns, especially in the current circumstances, and in this car. How in heaven's name did I miss it anyway?'

'Because, while you're obviously a pro, you're also something of a gentleman, James. You failed to grope the inside of my thighs when you frisked me in Cannobio.'

He recalled her flirtatious manner, and the cheeky smile. 'So, I suppose I'm now paying for the error. Are you going to tell me it's pointing at the back of my head?'

'Actually it's pointing towards my own left knee, back where it belongs. Not the most comfortable place to have a weapon.' She paused. 'Well, not *that* kind of a weapon anyway.'

A sign came up indicating a picnic area ahead. Bond slowed and pulled off the road, down a track through dense fir trees, and into a clearing. Rustic tables and benches stood in the centre. There was not a picnicker in sight. To one side a neat, clean, telephone box in working order awaited them.

Bond parked the car near the trees, ready for a quick getaway if necessary. He cut the engine, unfastened his seat belt, and turned to face Nannie Norrich, holding out his right hand, palm upwards.

'The gun, Nannie. I have to make a couple of important calls, and I'm not taking chances. Just give me the gun.'

Nannie smiled at him, a gentle, fond smile. 'You'd have to take it from me, James, and that might not be as easy as you imagine. Look, I used that weapon to help you. Sukie's given me my orders and I am going to co-operate. I can promise you, had she instructed otherwise, you would have known it very soon after my joining you.'

'Sukie's ordered you?' Bond felt lost.

'She's my boss. For the time being, anyway. I take orders from her, and . . .'

Sukie Tempesta put a hand on Bond's arm. 'I think I should explain, James. Nannie *is* an old school friend. She is also President of NUB.'

'And what the devil's the NUB?' Bond was cross now.

'Norrich Universal Bodyguards.'

'What?'

'Minders,' said Nannie, still very cheerful.

'Minders?' For a second he was incredulous.

'Minders, as in people who look after other people for money. Minders. Protectors.' Nannie began again: 'James, NUB is an all-women outfit, staffed by a special kind of woman. My girls are highly trained in weaponry, karate, all the martial arts, driving, flying – you name it, we do it. Truly, we're good, and we have a distinguished clientèle.'

'And Sukie Tempesta is among that clientèle?'

'Naturally. I always try to do that job myself.'

'Your people didn't do it very well the other evening in Belgium.' Bond heard the snarl in his voice. 'At the filling station. I ought to charge commission.'

Nannie sighed. 'It was unfortunate . . .'

'It was also my fault,' added Sukie. 'Nannie wanted to pick me up in Brussels, when her deputy had to leave. I said I'd get home without any trouble. I was wrong.'

'Of course you were wrong. Look, James, you've got problems. So has Sukie, mainly because she's a multimillionaire who insists on living in Rome for most of the year. She's a sitting duck. Go and make your telephone calls and just trust me. Trust us. Trust NUB.'

Eventually Bond shrugged, got out of the car and locked the two women in behind him. He took the CC500 from the boot and went over to the telephone booth. He made the slightly more complex attachments to link up the scrambler to the pay telephone. Then he dialled the operator, and placed a call to the Resident in Vienna.

The conversation was brief, and ended with the Resident agreeing to square with the Austrian police. He even suggested that a patrol meet Bond at the picnic area, if possible including the officer in charge of the May and Moneypenny kidnapping. 'Sit tight,' he advised. 'They should be with you in about an hour.'

Bond hung up, dialled the operator again, and within seconds was speaking to the Duty Officer at the Regent's Park Headquarters in London.

'Rome's men are dead,' the officer told him flatly. 'They were found in a ditch shot through the back of the head. Stay on the line. M wants a word.'

A moment later he heard his Chief's voice, sounding gruff. 'Bad business, James.' M called him James only in special circumstances.

'Very bad, sir. Moneypenny as well as my housekeeper missing.'

'Yes, and whoever has them is trying to strike a hard bargain.'

'Sir?'

'Nobody's told you?'

'I haven't seen anyone to speak to.'

There was a long pause. 'The women will be returned unharmed within forty-eight hours in exchange for you.'

'Ah,' said Bond, 'I thought it might be something like that. The Austrian police know of this?'

'I gather they have some of the details.'

'Then I'll hear it all when they arrive. I understand they're on their way. Please tell Rome I'm sorry about his two boys.'

'Take care, 007. We don't give in to terrorist demands in the Service. You know that, and you must abide by it. No heroics. No throwing your life away. You are not, repeat *not* to comply.'

'There may be no other way, sir.'

'There's always another way. Find it, and find it soon.' M closed the line.

Bond unhooked the CC500 and walked slowly back to the car. He knew that his life might be forfeit for those of May and Moneypenny. If there was no other way, then he would have to die. He also knew that he would go on to the bitter end, taking any risks that may resolve his dilemma.

It took exactly one hour and thirty-six minutes for the two police cars to arrive. While they waited, Nannie told Bond about the founding of Norrich Universal Bodyguards. In five years she had established branches in London, Paris, Rome, Los Angeles and New York, yet never once had she advertised the service.

'If I did, we'd get people thinking we were call girls. It's been a word-of-mouth thing from the start. What's more, it's fun.'

Bond wondered why neither he nor the Service had ever heard of them. NUB appeared to be a well kept secret within the close-knit circles of the ultra-rich.

'We don't often get spotted,' she told him. 'Men out with a girl minder look as though they're just on a date; and when I'm protecting a woman we make sure we both have safe men with us.' She laughed. 'I've seen poor Sukie through two dramatic love affairs in the last year alone.'

Sukie opened her mouth, her cheeks scarlet with fury, but at that moment, the police arrived. Two cars, their klaxons silent, swept into the glade in a cloud of dust. There were four uniformed officers in one car and three in the other, with a fourth in civilian clothes. The plain-clothes man unfolded himself from the back of the second car and thankfully stretched out his immense length. He was immaculately dressed, yet his frame was so badly proportioned that only an expert tailor could make him even half presentable. His arms were long, ending with very small hands that seemed to hang apelike almost down to his knees. His face, crowned with a head of gleaming hair, was too large for the oddly narrow shoulders. He had the apple cheeks of a fat farmer and a pair of great jug-handle ears.

'Oh, my God.' Nannie's whisper filled the interior of the Bentley with a breath of fear. 'Show your hands. Let them see your hands.' It was something Bond had already done instinctively.

'Der Haken!' Nannie whispered.

'The hook?' Bond hardly moved his lips.

'His real name's Inspektor Heinrich Osten. He's well over retirement age and stuck as an inspector, but he's the most ruthless, corrupt bastard in Austria.' She still whispered, as though the man who had now started to shamble towards them could hear every word. 'They say nobody's ever dared ask for his retirement because he knows too much about everyone – both sides of the law.'

'He knows you?' Bond asked.

'I've never met him. But he's on our files. The story is that as a very young man he was an ardent National Socialist. They call him Der Haken because he favoured a butcher's hook as a torture weapon. If we're dealing with this joker, we all need spoons a mile long. James, for God's sake don't trust him.'

Inspektor Osten had reached the Bentley and now stood with two uniformed men on Bond's side of the car. He stooped down, as though folding his body straight from the waist – reminding Bond of an oil pump – and waggled his small fingers outside the driver's window. They rippled, as though he were trying to attract the attention of a baby. Bond opened the window.

'Herr Bond?' The voice was thin and high-pitched.

'Yes. Bond. James Bond.'

'Good. We are to give you protection to Salzburg. Please to get out of your car for a moment.'

Bond opened the door, climbed out and looked up at the beaming polished-apple cheeks. He grasped the obscenely small hand, outstretched in greeting. It was like touching the dry skin of a snake.

'I am in charge of the case, Herr Bond. The case of the missing ladies – a good mystery title, *ja*?'

There was silence. Bond was not prepared to laugh at May's or Moneypenny's predicament.

'So,' the inspector became serious again. 'I am pleased to meet you. My name is Osten. Heinrich Osten.' His mouth opened in a grimace which revealed blackened teeth. 'Some people like to call me by another name. Der Haken. I do not know why, but it sticks. Probably it is because I hook out criminals.' He laughed again. 'I think, perhaps, I might even have hooked you, Herr Bond. The two of us have much to talk about. A great deal. I think I shall ride in your motor so we can talk. The ladies can go in the other cars.'

'No!' said Nannie sharply.

'Oh, but yes.'

Osten reached for the rear door and tugged it open. Already a uniformed man was half helping and half pulling Sukie from the passenger side. She and Nannie were dragged protesting and kicking to the other cars. Bond hoped Nannie had the sense not to reveal the .22. Then he realised how she would act. She would make a lot of noise, and in that way obtain legal freedom.

Osten gave his apple smile again. 'We shall talk better without the chatter of women, I think. In any case, Herr Bond, you do not wish them to hear me charge you with being an accessory to kidnapping and possibly murder, do you?'

7

THE HOOK

Bond drove with exaggerated care. For one thing, the sinister man who now sat next to him appeared to be possessed of a latent insanity which could explode into life at the slightest provocation. Bond had felt the presence of evil many times in his life, but now it was as strong as he could ever recall. The grotesque Inspektor Osten smelled of something else, and it took time to identify the old-fashioned bay rum which he obviously used in large quantities on his thatch of hair. They were several kilometres along the road before the silence was broken.

'Murder and kidnapping,' Osten said quietly, almost to himself.

'Blood sports,' Bond answered placidly. The policeman gave a low, rumbling chuckle.

'Blood sports is good, Mr Bond. Very good.'

'And you're going to charge me with them?'

'I can have you for murder,' Osten chuckled. 'You and the two young women. How do you say in England? On toast, I can have you.'

'I think you should check with your superiors before you try anything like that. In particular your own Department of Security and Intelligence.'

'Those skulking, prying idiots have little jurisdiction over me, Mr Bond.' Osten gave a short, contemptuous laugh.

'You're a law unto yourself, Inspektor?'

Osten sighed. Then, 'In this instance I am the law, and that's what matters. You have been concerned for two English ladies who have disappeared from a clinic . . .'

'One is a Scottish lady, Inspektor.'

'Whatever,' he raised a tiny doll's hand, the action at once dismissive and full of derision. 'You are the only key, the linking factor in this small mystery; the man who knew both victims. It is natural, then, that I must question you – interrogate you – thoroughly regarding these disappearances . . .'

'I've yet to learn the details myself. One of the ladies is my housekeeper . . .'

'The younger one?' The question was asked in a particularly unpleasant manner, and Bond replied with some asperity.

'No, Inspektor, the elderly Scottish lady. She's been with me for many years. The younger lady is a colleague. I think you should forget about interrogations until you hear from people of slightly higher status . . .'

'There are other matters – bringing a firearm into the country, a public shoot-out resulting in three deaths and great danger to innocent people using the autobahn . . .'

'With respect, the three men were trying to kill me and the two ladies who were in my car.'

Osten nodded, but with reservation. 'We shall see. In Salzburg we shall see.'

Casually, the man they called the Hook leaned over, his long arm stabbing forward, like a reptile, the tiny hand moving deftly. The inspector was not only experienced, Bond thought: he also had a highly developed intuition. Within seconds, he had removed both the ASP and the baton from their holsters.

'I am always uncomfortable with a man armed like this.' The apple cheeks puffed out like a balloon into a red shiny smile.

'If you look in my wallet, you'll find that I have an international licence to carry the gun,' Bond said, tightening his hands grimly on the wheel.

'We shall see.' Osten gave another sigh and repeated, 'In Salzburg we shall see.'

It was late when they reached the city, and Osten began to direct him peremptorily – left here, then right and another right. Bond caught a glimpse of the River Salzach, and the bridges crossing it. Behind him the Hohensalzburg castle, once the stronghold of the prince-archbishops, stood floodlit on its great mass of Dolomite rock, above the old town and river.

They were heading for the new town, and Bond expected to be guided towards the police headquarters. Instead, he found himself driving through a maze of streets, past a pair of modern apartment blocks and down into an underground car park. The two other cars, which they had lost on the outskirts of the city, were waiting, neatly parked with a space between them for the Bentley. Sukie sat in one, Nannie in the other.

A sudden uneasiness put Bond's senses on the alert. He had been assured by the Resident that the police were there to get him safely into Salzburg. Instead he was faced with a very unpleasant and probably corrupt policeman, and an apparently prearranged plan to bring them to a private building. He had no doubt that the car park belonged to an apartment block.

'Lower my window.' Osten spoke quietly.

One of the policemen had come over to Osten's side of the Bentley, and another stood in front of the vehicle. The second man had a machine pistol tucked into his hip, the evil eye of the muzzle pointing directly at Bond.

Through the open window, Osten muttered a few sentences of command in German. His voice was pitched so low, and his odd high-piping Viennese German so rapid that Bond caught only a few words: 'The women first', then a mutter, 'separate rooms . . . under guard at all times . . . until we have everything sorted out . . .' He ended with a question, which Bond did not catch at all. The answer, however, was clear.

'You are to telephone him as soon as possible.'

Heinrich Osten nodded his oversized head repeatedly, like a toy in a rear car window. He told the uniformed man to carry on. The one with the machine pistol did not move.

'We sit quietly for a few minutes.' The head turned towards Bond, red cheeks puffed in a smile.

'As you have only hinted at charges against me, I think I should be allowed to speak to my Embassy in Vienna.' Bond clipped out the words, as though they were parade ground orders.

'All in good time. There are formalities.' Osten sat supremely calm, his hands folded as though in complete command of the situation.

'Formalities? What formalities?' Bond shouted. 'People have rights. In particular, I am on an official assignment. I demand to . . .'

Osten gave the hint of a nod towards the policeman with the machine pistol. 'You can demand nothing, Mr Bond. Surely you understand that. You are a stranger in a strange land. By the very fact that I am the representative of the law, and you have an Uzi trained on you, you have no rights.'

Bond watched Sukie and Nannie being hustled from the other cars. They were kept well apart from one another. Both looked frightened. Sukie did not even turn her head in the direction of the Bentley, but Nannie glanced towards him. In an instant the message was clear in her eyes. She was still armed and biding her time. A remarkably tough lady, he thought: tough and attractive in a clean-scrubbed kind of way.

The women disappeared from Bond's line of vision, and a moment later Osten prodded him in the ribs with his own ASP.

'Leave the keys in the car, Mr Bond. It has to be moved from here before the morning. Just get out, showing your hands the whole time. My officer with the Uzi is a little nervous.'

Bond did as he was bid. The nearly deserted underground park felt cool and eerie, smelling of gasoline, rubber and oil.

The man with the machine pistol motioned to him to walk between the other cars to a small exit passage, and towards what appeared to be a brick wall. Osten made a slight movement, and Bond caught sight of a flat remote control in his left hand.

Silently a door-sized section of the brickwork moved inwards and then slid to one side, revealing steel elevator doors. Somewhere in the car park an engine fired, throbbed and settled as a vehicle made its exit.

The elevator arrived with a brief sigh, and Bond was signalled to enter. The three men stood without speaking as the lift cage made its noiseless upward journey. The doors slid open and again Bond was ushered forward, this time into a passageway lined with modern prints. A second later they were in a large, luxurious apartment. The carpets were Turkish, the furnishings modern, in wood, steel, glass and expensive fabrics. On the walls were paintings and drawings by Piper, Sutherland, Bonnard, Gross and Hockney. From the enormous open-plan room, plate-glass windows led to a wide balcony. To the left, an archway revealed the dining area and kitchen. From lower arches ran two long passages with gleaming white doors on either side. A police officer stood in each of these as though on guard. Outside a floodlit Hohensalzburg could be seen before Osten ordered the curtains to be closed. Light blue velvet slid along soundless rails.

'Nice little place you have for a police inspector,' Bond said.

'Ah, my friend. I wish it were mine. I have only borrowed it for this one evening.'

Bond nodded, trying to indicate this was obvious, if only because of the style and elegance. He turned to face the inspector, and began speaking rapidly. 'Now, sir. I appreciate what you've told me, but you must know that our Embassy and the department I represent have already given instructions as to my safety, and received assurances from your own people. You say I have no right to demand anything, but you make a grave error there. In fact I have the right to demand everything.'

Der Haken looked at him glassy-eyed, then gave a loud chuckle. 'If you were alive, Mr Bond. Yes, if you were still alive you would have the right, and I would have the duty to co-operate if I were also alive. Unhappily we are both dead men.'

Bond scowled, just beginning to appreciate what Osten intended.

'The problem is actually yours,' the policeman continued. 'For you really are a dead man. I am merely lying – what is the phrase? Lying doggo?'

'A little old-fashioned, but it'll do.'

Osten smiled and glanced around him. 'I shall be living in this kind of world very shortly. A good place for a ghost, yes?'

'Enchanting. And what kind of place will I be haunting?'

Any trace of humanity disappeared from the policeman's face. The muscles turned to hard rock, and the glassy stare broke and splintered. Even the apple cheeks seemed to lose colour and become sallow.

'The grave, Mr Bond. You will be haunting the cold, cold grave. You will be nowhere. Nothing. It will be as though you had never existed.' His small hand flicked up so that he could glance at his wrist watch, and he turned to the man with the Uzi, sharply ordering him to switch on the television. 'The late news will be starting any moment. My death should already have been reported. Yours will be announced as probable – though it will be more than probable before dawn. Please sit down and watch. I think you'll agree that my improvisation has been brilliant, for I only had a very short time to set things up.'

Bond slumped into a chair, half his mind on the chances of dealing with Osten and his accomplices, the other half working out what the policeman had planned and why.

There were commercials on the big colour screen. Attractive Austrian girls standing against mountain scenery told the world of the essential value of a sun barrier cream. A young man arrived hatless from the air, climbed from his light aircraft and said the view was *wunderschön* but even more *wunderschön* when you used a certain kind of camera to capture it.

The news graphics filled the screen and a serious-faced brunette appeared. The lead story was about a shooting incident on the A12 autobahn. One car carrying tourists had been fired at and had crashed in flames. The pictures showed the wreckage of the silver Renault surrounded by police and ambulances. The young woman, now looking very grave, appeared again. The horror had been compounded by the death of five police officers in a freak accident as they sped from Salzburg to the scene of the shooting. One of the police cars had gone out of control and was hit broadside on by the other. Both cars had skidded into woodland and caught fire.

There were more pictures showing the remains of the two cars. Then Inspektor Heinrich Osten's official photograph came up in black and white, and the newscaster said that Austria had lost one of her most efficient and long-serving officers. The inspector had been travelling in the second car and had died of multiple burns.

Next Bond saw his own photograph and the number plate of the Bentley Mulsanne Turbo. He was said to be a British diplomat, travelling on private business, probably with two unidentified young women. He was wanted for questioning regarding the original shooting incident. A statement from the Embassy said he had telephoned appealing for help, but they feared he might have been affected by stress and run amok. 'He has been under great strain during the last few days,' a bland Embassy spokesman told a television reporter. So, the Service and Foreign Office had decided to deny him. Well, that was standard. The car, diplomat and young women had disappeared and there were fears for their lives. The police would resume the search at daybreak, but the car could easily have gone off one of the mountain roads. The worst was feared.

Der Haken began to laugh. 'You see how simple it all is, Mr Bond? When they find your car smashed to pieces at the bottom of a ravine sometime tomorrow, the search will be over. There will be three mutilated bodies inside.'

The full impact of the inspector's plan had struck home.

'Mine will be without its head, I presume?' Bond asked calmly.

'Naturally,' Der Haken said with a scowl. 'It seems you know what's going on.'

'I know that somehow you've managed to murder five of your colleagues . . .'

The tiny hand came up. 'No! No! Not my colleagues, Mr Bond. Tramps, vagrants. Scum. Yes, we cleaned up some scum . . .'

'With two extra police cars?'

'With the two original police cars. The ones in the garage are fakes. I have kept a pair of white VWs with detachable police decals and plates for a long time, in case I should need them. The moment arrived suddenly.'

'Yesterday?'

'When I discovered the real reason for the kidnapping of your friends – and the reward. Yes, it was yesterday. I have ways and means of contacting people. Once I knew about the ransom demand I made enquiries and came up with . . .'

'The Head Hunt.'

'Precisely. You're very well informed. The people offering the large prize gave me the impression that you were in the dark – that is correct, in the dark?'

'For a late starter, Inspektor, you seem to be well organised,' said Bond.

'Ach! Organised!' The polished cheeks blossomed with pride. 'I have spent most of my life being ready to move at short notice – with ways, means, papers, friends, transport.'

Clearly the man was very sure of himself, as well he might be, with Bond captive in a building high above Salzburg, his own territory. He was also expansive.

'I have always known the chance of real wealth and escape would come through something big like a blackmail or kidnap case. The petty criminals could never supply me with the kind of money I really need to be independent. If I was able to do a private deal, in, as I have said, a blackmail, or kidnap, case, then my last years were secure. But I never in my craziest dreams expected the riches that have come with you, Mr Bond.' He

beamed like a malicious child. 'In my time here I have made
sure that my team had the proper incentives. Now they have a
great and always good reason for helping me. They're not really
uniformed men, of course. They are my detective squad. But
they would die for me . . .'

'Or for the money,' Bond said coldly. 'They might even dispose of you for the money.'

Der Haken laughed shortly. 'You have to be up early in the
morning to catch an old bird like me, Mr Bond. They could try to
kill me, I suppose, but I doubt it. What I do not doubt is that
they will help me to dispose of you.' He rose. 'You will excuse
me, I have an important telephone call to make.'

Bond lifted a hand. 'Inspektor! One favour! The two young
women are here?'

'Naturally.'

'They have nothing to do with me. We met entirely by
chance. They're not involved, so I ask you to let them go.'

Der Haken did not even look at Bond as he muttered, 'Impossible', and strode off down one of the passageways.

The man with the Uzi smiled at Bond over the barrel, then
spoke in bad English. 'He is very clever, Der Haken, yes? Always
he promises us one day there will be a way to make us all rich.
Now he says we will sit in sunshine and luxury soon.' Like as
not, Osten would see his four accomplices at the bottom of some
ravine before he made off with the reward – if he ever got the
reward. In German he asked how they had concocted a plan so
quickly.

Der Haken's team had been working on the kidnapping at the
Klinik Mozart. There were a lot of telephone calls. Suddenly the
inspector disappeared for about an hour. He returned jubilant.
He had brought the whole team to this apartment and explained
the situation. All they had to do was catch a man called Bond.
The accident was simple to stage. Once they had him, the
kidnapping would be over – only there was a bonus. The people

who owned this very apartment would see that the women were returned to the clinic and pay a huge sum for Bond's head.

'The Inspektor kept calling in to headquarters,' the man told him. 'He was trying to find out where you were. When he discovered, we left in the cars. We were already on the way when the radio call told us you were waiting off the A8. There had been shooting and a car was destroyed. He thinks on his feet, the Inspektor. We picked up five vagrants, from the worst area of the town, and drove them to the place where we keep the other cars. The rest was easy. We had uniforms with the cars; the vagrants were drunk and easy to make completely unconscious. Then we came on to pick you up.' He was not certain of the next moves in the game, but knew his chief would get the money. At that moment Der Haken strode back into the room.

'It is all arranged,' he said, smiling. 'I am afraid I shall have to lock you in one of the rooms, like the others, Mr Bond. But only for an hour or two. I have a visitor. When my visitor has gone we will all go for a short drive into the mountains. The Head Hunt is almost over.'

Bond nodded, thinking to himself that the Head Hunt was not almost over. There were always ways. He now had to find a way quickly to get them all out of Der Haken's clutches. The grotesque inspector was gesturing with the ASP, indicating that Bond should go down the passageway on the right. Bond took a step towards the arch, then stopped.

'Two questions. Last requests, if you like . . .'

'The women have to go,' Osten said quietly. 'I cannot keep witnesses.'

'And I would do the same in your shoes. I understand. No, my questions are merely to ease my own mind. First, who were the men in the Renault? They were obviously taking part in this bizarre hunt for my head. I'd like to know.'

'Union Corse, so I understand,' Der Haken was in a hurry, agitated, as though his visitor would arrive at any moment.

'And what happened to my housekeeper and Miss Money-penny?'

'Happened? They were kidnapped.'

'Yes, but how did it take place?'

Der Haken gave a snarl of irritation. 'I haven't got time to go into details now. They were kidnapped. You do not need to know anything else.' He gave Bond a light push, heading him in the direction of the passage. At the third door on the right Der Haken stopped, unlocked it and almost threw Bond inside. He heard the key turn and the lock thud home.

Bond found himself in a bright bedroom with a modern four poster, more expensive prints, an armchair, dressing table and built-in wardrobe. The single window was draped with heavy cream curtains.

He moved quickly, first checking the casement window, which looked out on to a narrow section of balcony at the side of the building – almost certainly part of the large main terrace. The glass was thick, unbreakable, and the locks were high-security and would take time to remove. An assault on the door was out of the question. There was a deadlock on it that wouldn't be easy to break without a lot of noise and the only tools he had hidden on him were small. At a pinch he might just do the window, but what then? He was at least six storeys above ground. He was also unarmed and without any climbing aids.

He checked the wardrobe and dressing table; every drawer and cupboard in the room was empty. As he did so, a door bell sounded from far away in the main area of the apartment. The visitor had arrived – Tamil Rahani's emissary, he supposed; certainly someone of authority in SPECTRE. Time was running out. It would have to be the window.

Oddly for a policeman, Osten had left him with his belt. Hidden almost undetectably between the thick layers of leather was the long, thin multi-purpose tool, made like a very slim Swiss Army knife. Fashioned in toughened steel, it contained a whole set of minute tools – screwdrivers, picklocks, even a tiny battery and connectors which could be used in conjunction with three small explosive charges, the size and thickness of a fingernail, hidden in the casing.

The Toolkit had been designed by Major Boothroyd's brilliant assistant in Q Branch, Anne Reilly known to everyone at the Regent's Park Headquarters as Q'ute. Bond silently blessed her ingenuity as he now set to work on the security locks screwed tightly into the casement frame. There were two, in addition to the lock on the handle, and it took about ten minutes to remove the first of these. At this rate of progress, there was at least another twenty minutes work – possibly more – and Bond guessed he didn't have that kind of time at his disposal.

He worked on, blistering and grazing his fingers, knowing the alternative of trying to blow the deadlock on the door was a futile exercise. They would cut him down almost before he could reach the passage.

From time to time he stopped, listening for any noise coming from the main room in the apartment. Not a sound reached him, and he finally disposed of the second lock. All that remained was the catch on the handle, and he had just started to work on it when a blaze of light came on outside. Somebody had switched on the balcony lights and one was on the wall just outside this bedroom window.

He could still hear nothing. The place probably had some soundproofing in the walls, while the windows were so toughened that little noise from outside would seep through. After a few seconds, his eyes adjusted to the new light and he was able to continue his attack on the main lock. Five minutes passed before he managed to get one screw off. He stopped, leaned against the wall and decided to have a go at the lock mechanism itself, which held down the catch and handle.

He tried three different picklocks before hitting on the right one. There was a sharp click as the bar slid back. A glance at his Rolex told him the whole business had taken over forty-five minutes. There could be very little time left, and he still had no firm plan in mind.

Quietly Bond lifted the handle and pulled the window in towards him. It did not squeak, but a chill blast of air hit him and he took several deep breaths to clear his head. He stood, ears straining for any sound that might come from the main terrace round the corner to his right.

There was only silence.

Bond was puzzled. Time must now be running out for Der Haken. It had long been obvious that one of the competitors was watching, waiting for the moment to strike, carefully taking out the opposition as he went along. Der Haken had arrived, unexpectedly, on the scene. He was the wild card, the joker – the outsider who had suddenly solved SPECTRE's problems. He would have to move fast to ensure his reward.

Carefully, making no noise, Bond eased his way through the window and pressed against the wall. Still there was no sound. Cautiously he peered round the corner of the building to the wide terrace, high above Salzburg. It was furnished with lamps, huge pots filled with flowers and white-painted garden furniture. Even Bond took in a quick, startled breath as he looked at the scene. The lamps blazed and the panorama of the new and old towns twinkled as a beautiful backdrop. The furniture was neatly arranged – as were the corpses.

Der Haken's four accomplices had been laid out in a row between the white wrought-iron chairs, each man with the top of his head blown away, the blood stippling the furnishings and walls, seeping out over the flagstones set into the thick concrete balcony.

Above the huge sliding windows leading to the main room pots of scarlet geraniums hung on hooks embedded in the wall. One of these had been removed and in its place was a rope with a small reinforced loop. A long, sharp butcher's hook was threaded through the loop, and on its great spike Der Haken himself had been hung.

Bond wondered when he had last witnessed a sight as revolting as this. The policeman's hands and feet were tied together, and the point of the hook had been pushed into his throat. It was long enough to have penetrated the roof of the mouth, and to re-emerge through the left eye. Someone had taken great trouble to see that the big, ungainly man had suffered slowly and unremittingly. If the old Nazi stories were true, then whoever had done this wanted Inspektor Heinrich Osten's death to be seen as poetic justice.

The body, still dripping blood, swung slightly in the breeze, the neck stretching almost visibly as it moved. What was left of the face was contorted in horrible agony.

Bond swallowed and stepped towards the window. At that moment there came a grotesque background sound, mingling with the creaking of rope on hook. From across the street, a group of rehearsing musicians began to play. Mozart, naturally; Bond thought it was the sombre opening of the Piano Concerto No. 20, but his knowledge of Mozart was limited. Then farther down the street a jazz trumpeter, a busker probably, started up. It was an odd counterpoint, the Concerto mingling with the 1930s' *Big House Blues*. Bond wondered if it were mere coincidence.

8

UNDER DISCIPLINE

Bond needed time to think, but standing there on the terrace amidst the carnage was not conducive to concentration. It was now three o'clock in the morning. Apart from the music floating up from below, the city of Salzburg was silent – a glitter of lights, with the outline of mountains showing pitch black against the dark navy sky.

The lights were still on in the main room as he entered. There was no sign of a struggle. Whoever had blown away Der Haken and his crew must have operated very quickly. There would have been more than one to deal with those five men. And whoever had carried out the executions would have been trusted, at least by Osten. Bloodstains could be seen on the wall between the two archways, and there were more traces on the deep pile cream carpet. On one of the tables his ASP and baton lay in full view. Bond checked the weapon, which was still loaded and unfired, before returning it to the holster. He paused, weighing the baton for a moment before slipping it into the cylindrical holder still attached to his belt.

Then he went over and closed the windows, Der Haken's body bumping heavily against the glass, and found the button which operated the curtains, blotting out the gruesome sight on the terrace.

He had moved from the balcony quickly, knowing that whoever had finished off the policemen could still be in the apartment. Drawing the ASP, Bond began a systematic search of the flat. The door out to the lift appeared to have been secured from the outside, and three of the rooms were also firmly locked. One was the guest room he had recently vacated, the other two, he deduced, contained Sukie and Nannie. There was no response from either room when he knocked, and no sign of keys.

Two things worried Bond. Why, with his quarry under lock and key in this very apartment, had not his adversary used the opportunity to kill him on the spot? One of the Head Hunt competitors appeared to be playing a devious game and eliminating any other competitor who had come near the prize. Who were the most likely people to be running this kind of interference? The obvious choice was SPECTRE itself. It would be just their style to mount a competition with a fabulous price on the victim's head, and then step in at the last moment to reap the reward. That would be the most economic way to have your cake and eat it.

But if SPECTRE were responsible for knocking out the opposition, they surely would have disposed of him by now? Who could be left in the game? Perhaps one of the unsympathetic espionage organisations? If so, Bond's first choice would be the current successors to his old enemy, SMERSH.

Since he had first encountered this devious arm of the KGB, SMERSH (an acronym for *Smiert Spionam:* Death to Spies) had undergone a whole series of changes. For many years it had been known as Department Thirteen, before becoming completely independent as Department V. In fact, Bond's Service had allowed all but their inner circle to go on referring to Department V long after it too had disappeared.

What had happened was very much the concern of the Secret Intelligence Service, who had been running an agent of their own, Oleg Lyalin, deep within Department V. When Lyalin defected in the early 1970s, it took a little time for the KGB to discover he had been a long-term mole. After that Department V had suffered a purge which virtually put it out of business.

Even Bond had not been informed until relatively recently

that his old enemies were now completely reformed under the title Department Eight of Directorate S. Was this new KGB operations unit now the likeliest dark horse in the race for his head?

In the meantime, there were very pressing problems. Check out the rooms which he thought contained Nannie and Sukie; and do something about getting out of the apartment block. The Bentley Mulsanne Turbo cannot be called the most discreet of vehicles. Bond reckoned that, with the alert still on, he could get about half a kilometre before being picked up.

Searching Der Haken's swinging body was not pleasant, but it did yield the Bentley keys, but not those to the guest bedrooms or to the elevator.

The telephone was still working, but Bond had no way of making a clandestine call. Carefully he dialled the direct number for the Service Resident in Vienna. It rang nine times before a befuddled voice responded.

'It's Predator,' Bond said quickly, using his field cryptonym. 'I have to speak clearly, even if the Pope himself has a wire on your telephone.'

'Do you realise it's three in the morning? Where the hell are you? There's been an almighty fuss. A senior Austrian police officer . . .'

'And four of his friends were killed,' Bond interrupted.

'They're out looking for you . . . How did you know about the policeman?'

'Because he didn't get killed . . .'

'What?'

'The bastard was doubling. Set it up himself.'

'Where are you?' The Resident now sounded concerned.

'Somewhere in the new town, in a very plush apartment block, together with five corpses and, I hope, the two young ladies who were with me. I haven't a clue about the address, but there's a telephone number you can work from.' He read out the number on the handset.

'Enough to be going on with. I'll call you back as soon as I get something sorted out, though I suspect you're going to be asked a lot of questions.'

'The hell with the questions, just let me get out to the clinic and on with the job. Quickly as you can.'

Bond closed the line. He then went to the first of the two locked rooms and banged hard on the door. This time he thought he could hear muffled grunts coming from inside. The deadlock would have to be dealt with by brute force, whatever the noise.

In the kitchen he found a sharp, heavy meat cleaver, with which he demolished a section of door round the lock. Sukie Tempesta lay on the bed, bound, gagged, and stripped to her plain underwear.

'They took my clothes!' she shouted angrily when he got the ropes untied and the gag off.

'So I see,' Bond said with a smile as she reached for a blanket.

He went across to the other room, where he succeeded in breaking in more quickly. Nannie was in the same situation, only she looked as though she bought her underwear from Fredericks of Hollywood. It was always the plain-looking ones, Bond thought, as she yelled,

'They took my suspender belt with the holster on it.'

At that moment the telephone started to ring. Bond lifted the receiver.

'Predator.'

'A very senior officer's on the way with a team,' the Resident said. 'For heaven's sake be discreet, and tell only what is absolutely necessary. Then get to Vienna as fast as you can. That's an order from on high.'

'Tell them to bring women's clothes,' Bond snapped, giving a rough estimate of the sizes.

By the time he was off the telephone he could hear squeals of delight from one of the bathrooms, where the clothes had been found bundled into a cupboard. Sukie came through fully dressed but, almost blatantly, Nannie appeared doing up her stockings to her retrieved suspender belt, which still had holster and pistol in place.

'Let's get some air in here,' Sukie said, advancing towards the windows. Bond stepped in front of her, saying that he would not advise even opening the curtains, let alone the windows. Quietly, he explained why and told them to stay in the main room. Then he made his own way behind the drapes to let air into the room.

The doorbell rang violently. After shouted identifications, Bond explained in German through the closed door that he could not get it open from inside. He heard sets of keys rattling as they were tried in the lock before the seventh worked and the door swung open to admit what seemed like half the Salzburg police force, headed by a smart, authoritative, grey-haired man whom the rest treated with great respect. He introduced himself as Kommissar Becker. The investigative team got on with their job on the terrace while Becker talked to Bond. Sukie and Nannie were led away by plain-clothes men, presumably to be questioned separately elsewhere.

Becker had a long patrician nose and kindly eyes. He knew the score and came quickly to the point.

'I have been instructed by our Foreign Ministry and Security Departments,' he began in almost unaccented English. 'I understand that the Head of the Service to which you belong has also been in touch. All I want from you is a detailed statement. You will then be free to go. But, Mr Bond, I think it would be advisable for you to be out of Austria within twenty-four hours.'

'Is that official?'

Becker shook his head. 'No, not official. It is merely my own opinion. Something I would advise. Now, Mr Bond, let us take it from the top as they say in musical circles.'

Bond recounted the story, omitting all he knew about Tamil Rahani and SPECTRE's Head Hunt. He passed off the shoot-out on the autobahn as one of those occupational hazards that can befall anyone involved in his kind of clandestine work.

'There is no need to be shy about your status,' Becker said with an avuncular smile. 'In our police work here in Austria, we come into contact with all kinds of strange people, from many walks of life – American, British, French, German and Russian – if you follow me. We are almost a clearing house for spies, only I know you don't like to use that word.'

'It is rather old-hat.' Bond found himself smiling back. 'In many ways we are an outdated tribe and a lot of people would like to see us consigned to the scrap heap. Satellites and computers have taken over much of our work.'

'It is the same with us,' the policeman said with a shrug. 'However, nothing can replace the policeman on the beat, and I'm sure there is still a need for the man on the ground in your business. It is the same in war also. However many tactical or strategic missiles appear over the horizon the military needs live bodies in the field. Here we are geographically placed at a dangerous crossroads. We have a saying especially for the NATO powers. If the Russians come, they will be in Vienna for breakfast; but they will have their afternoon tea in London.'

With a detective's knack of moving from a digression back to the mainstream of questioning, Becker asked about the motives of Heinrich Osten – Der Haken – and Bond gave him a word by word account of what had passed between them, again leaving out the core of the business concerning the Head Hunt.

'He has apparently been looking for a chance to line his pockets, and get away, for many years.'

Becker gave a wry smile. 'It doesn't surprise me. Der Haken, as most people called him, had an odd hold over the authorities. There are still many folk, some in high office, who recall the old days, the Nazis. They remember Osten all too well, I fear. Whoever brought him to this unpleasant end has done us a favour.' Again, he switched his tack. 'Tell me, why do you think the ransom has been set so high on the two ladies?'

He tried his innocent expression. 'I don't really know the terms of the ransom. In fact, I have yet to be told the full story of the kidnapping.'

Becker repeated his wry smile, this time wagging a finger as though Bond were a naughty schoolboy. 'Oh, I believe you know the terms well enough. After all, you were in Osten's company for some time after the reports of his death. I took over the case last night. The ransom is you, Mr Bond, and you know it. There's also the little matter of ten million Swiss francs lying, literally, on your head.'

Bond made a gesture of capitulation. 'Okay, so the hostages are being held against me, and your colleague found out about the contract, which is worth a lot of money . . .'

'Even if you had been responsible for his death,' Becker cut in, 'I don't think many police officers, either here or in Vienna, would go out of their way to charge you – Der Haken being what he was.' He lifted an inquisitorial eyebrow. 'You didn't kill him, did you?'

'You've had the truth from me. No, I didn't, but I think I know who did.'

'Without even knowing the details of the kidnapping?' Becker enquired sagely.

'Yes. Miss May – my housekeeper – and Miss Moneypenny are bait. As you say, it's me they want. These people know I will do everything I can to rescue the ladies, and that in the last resort I'd give myself up to save them.'

'You are prepared to give your life for an elderly spinster and a colleague of uncertain age?'

'Also a spinster,' Bond said with a smile. 'The answer is yes, I would do that – though I intend to do it without losing my head.'

'My information is, Mr Bond, that you have many times almost lost your head over . . .'

'What we used to call a bit of fluff?' Bond smiled again.

'That is an expression I do not know – bit of fluff.'

'Bit of fluff, piece of skirt – young woman,' Bond explained.

'Yes. Yes, I see, and you are correct. Our records show you as a veritable St George slaying dragons to save young and attractive women. This is an unusual situation for you. I . . .'

Bond cut in sharply, 'Can you tell me what actually happened? How the kidnap took place?'

Kommissar Becker paused as a plain-clothes officer came into the room and there was a quick exchange. The officer told Becker that the women had been questioned. Becker instructed him to wait with them for a short time. The team on the balcony were also completing their preliminary investigation.

'Inspektor Osten's case notes are somewhat hazy,' the Kommissar said. 'But we do have a few details, of his interviews with Herr Doktor Kirchtum of the Klinik Mozart, and others.'

'Well?'

'Well, it appears that your colleague, Miss Moneypenny, visited the patient twice. After the second occasion she telephoned the Herr Direktor asking permission to take Miss May out – to a concert. It seemed a pleasant and untaxing suggestion. The doctor gave his consent. Miss Moneypenny arrived as arranged in a chauffeur driven car. There was another man with her.'

'There is a description?'

'The car was a BMW . . .'

'The man?'

'A silver BMW, a Series 7. The chauffeur was in uniform, and the man went into the clinic with Miss Moneypenny. The staff who saw them said he was in his mid-thirties, with light hair, and was well dressed, tall and muscular.'

'And Miss Moneypenny's behaviour?'

'She was a little edgy, a tiny bit nervous. Miss May was in good spirits. One nurse noticed that Miss Moneypenny treated her with great care. The nurse said it was as though your Miss Moneypenny had nursing experience. She also had the impression that the young man knew something about medicine.

He stayed very close to Miss May the whole time.' The policeman drew in breath through his teeth. 'They got into the BMW
and drove off. Four hours later, Herr Doktor Kirchtum received a
telephone call saying they had been abducted. You know the
rest.'

'I do?' Bond asked.

'You were told. You started out towards Salzburg. Then there
were the shoot-out and your unpleasant experience with Inspektor Osten.'

'What about the car? The BMW?'

'It has not been sighted, which means that either it was out of
Austria very quickly with the plates changed and maybe a
respray, or it's hidden away somewhere until all goes quiet.'

'And there's nothing else?'

It was as though the Kommissar was holding something back,
uncertain whether to speak. He did not look at Bond but towards
the men on the balcony, taking their photographs and measure-
ments.

'Yes. Yes, there is one other thing. It was not in Osten's notes,
but they had it on the general file at headquarters.'

He hesitated again, and Bond had to prompt him. 'What was
on file?'

'At 15.10 on the afternoon of the kidnapping – that is, around
three hours before it took place – Austrian Airlines received a
last-minute booking from the Klinik Mozart. The caller said they
had two very sick ladies who had to be transported to Frankfurt.
There is a flight at 19.05, OS 421, which arrives at Frankfurt at
20.15. That evening there were few passengers so the booking
was accepted.'

'And the ladies made the flight?'

'They went first class. On stretchers. They were unconscious,
and their faces were covered with bandages . . .'

A classic KGB ploy, thought Bond. They had been doing it for
years. He recalled the famous Turkish incident, and there had
been two at Heathrow.

'They were accompanied,' Kommissar Becker continued, 'by two nurses and a doctor. The doctor was a young, tall, good-looking man with fair hair.'

Bond nodded. 'And further enquiries showed that no such reservation had been made from the Klinik Mozart.'

'Exactly.' The Kommissar raised his eyebrows. 'One of our men followed up the booking on his own initiative. Certainly Inspektor Osten did not instruct him to do it.'

'And?'

'They were met by a genuine ambulance team at Frankfurt. They transferred on to another flight, the Air France 749, arriving in Paris at 21.30. It left Frankfurt on schedule, at 20.25. The ambulance people just had time to complete the transfer. We know nothing about what happened at the Paris end, but the kidnap call was placed to Doktor Kirchtum at 21.45. So they admitted the abduction as soon as the victims were safely away.'

'Paris,' Bond repeated absently. 'Why Paris?'

As though in answer to his question, the telephone began to ring. Becker himself picked it up and said nothing, but waited for an identification on the line. His eyes flicked towards Bond, betraying signs of alarm.

'For you,' he mouthed quietly, handing over the mouthpiece. 'The Herr Doktor Kirchtum.'

Bond took the handset and identified himself. Kirchtum's voice still held its resonance, but he was obviously a very frightened man. There was a distinct tremor in his tone, and there were pauses between his words, as though he was being prompted.

'Herr Bond,' he began, 'Herr Bond, I have a gun . . . They have a gun . . . It is in my left ear, and they say they will pull the trigger if I don't give you the correct message.'

'Go on,' Bond said calmly.

'They know you are with the police. They know you have been ordered to go to Vienna. That is what I must first tell you.'

So, Bond thought, they had a wire on this telephone and had listened to his call to the Resident in Vienna.

Kirchtum continued very shakily. 'You are not to tell the police of your movements.'

'No. Okay. What am I to do?'

'They say they have booked a room for you at the Goldener Hirsch . . .'

'That's impossible. You have to book months ahead . . .'

The quaver in Kirchtum's voice became more pronounced. 'I assure you, Herr Bond, for these people nothing is impossible. They understand you have two ladies with you. They say they have a room reserved for them also. It is not the fault of the ladies that they have been . . . have been . . . I'm sorry, I cannot read the writing . . . Ah, have been implicated. For the time being these ladies will stay at the Goldener Hirsch, you understand?'

'I understand.'

'You will stay there and await instructions. You will tell the police to keep away from you. You will on no account contact your people in London, not even through your man in Vienna. I am to ask if this is understood?'

'It is understood.'

'They say, good, because if it is not understood, Miss May and her friend will depart, and not peacefully.'

'It is *understood!*' Bond shouted in the mouthpiece.

There was a moment's silence. 'The gentlemen here wish to play a tape for you. Are you ready?'

'Go ahead.'

There was a click at the other end of the line. Then Bond heard May's voice, unsteady, but still the same old May.

'Mr James, some foreign friends of yorn, seem to hae the idea that I can be afeard easy. Dinna worry aboot me, Mr Jam . . .' There was a sudden slap as a hand went over her mouth, then Moneypenny's voice, thick with fear, sounded as clear as if she were standing behind him. 'James!' she cried. 'Oh, God, James . . . James . . .'

Suddenly an unearthly scream cut into his ear – loud and terrified, and obviously coming from May. It made Bond's blood run cold. It was enough to place him in the power of those holding the two women captive, for it would take something truly terrifying to make tough old May scream like that. Bond was ready to obey them to the death.

He looked up. Becker was staring at him. 'For pity's sake, Kommissar, you didn't hear any of that conversation.'

'What conversation?' Becker's expression did not change.

9

VAMPIRE

Salzburg was crowded – a large number of American citizens were out to see Europe before they died, and an equally large number of Europeans were out to see Europe before it completely changed into Main Street Common Market. Many thought they were already too late, but Salzburg, with the ghost of Mozart, and its own particular charm, did better than most.

The hotel Goldener Hirsch holds up exceptionally well, especially as its charm, comfort and hospitality reaches a long arm back through eight hundred years.

They had to use one of the festival car parks and carry their luggage to the Goldener Hirsch, where it stands in the traffic-free centre of the old town, close to the crowded, colourful Getreidegasse with its exquisite carved window frames and gilded wrought iron shop signs.

'How in the name of Blessed St Michael did you get reservations at the Goldener Hirsch?' asked Nannie.

'Influence,' Bond said soberly. 'Why St Michael?'

'Michael the Archangel. Patron saint of bodyguards and minders.'

Bond thought grimly that he needed all the help the angels could provide. Heaven alone knew what instructions he would receive within the next twenty-four hours, or whether they would be in the form of a bullet or a knife.

Before they left the Bentley, Nannie cleared her throat.

'James,' she began primly, 'you said something a while back that Sukie finds offensive, and doesn't make me happy either.'

'Oh?'

'You said we'd only have to bear with you for another twenty-four hours or so.'

'Well, it's true.'

'No! No, it isn't true.'

'I was accidentally forced to involve you both in a potentially very dangerous situation. I had no option but to drag you into it. You've both been courageous, and a great help, but it couldn't have been fun. What I'm telling you now is that you'll both be out of it within twenty-four hours or so.'

'We don't want to be out of it,' Nannie said calmly.

'Yes, it's been hairy,' Sukie began, 'but we feel that we're your friends. You're in trouble, and . . .'

'Sukie's instructed me to remain with you. To mind you, James, and, while I'm at it, she's coming along for the ride.'

'That just might not be possible.' Bond looked at each girl in turn, his clear blue eyes hard and commanding.

'Well, it'll just have to become possible.' Sukie was equally determined.

'Look, Sukie, it's quite likely that I shall be given instructions from a very persuasive authority. They may well demand that you're left behind, released, ordered to go your own sweet way.'

Nannie was just as firm. 'Well, it's just too bad if our own sweet way happens to be the same as your own sweet way, James. That's all there is to it.'

Bond shrugged. Time would tell. It was possible that he would be ordered to take the women with him anyway, as hostages. If not, there should be an opportunity to leave quietly when the time came. The third option was that it would all end here, at the Goldener Hirsch, in which case the question would not arise.

'I might need some stamps,' Bond said, quietly, to Sukie as they approached the hotel. 'Quite a lot. Enough for a small package to the UK. Could you get them? Send a few innocuous postcards by the porter, and collect some stamps at the same time if you would.'

'Of course, James,' she answered.

The Goldener Hirsch is said by many to be the best hotel in Salzburg – enchanting, elegant and picturesque, even if rather self-consciously so. The staff are dressed in the local Loden and the rooms are heavy with Austrian history. Bond reflected that his room could have been prepared for the shooting of *The Sound of Music*.

As the porter left, closing the door discreetly behind him, Bond heard Kirchtum's warning again clear in his head: 'You will . . . await instructions . . . You will on no account contact your people in London.' So, for the time being at least, it would be folly to telephone London, or even Vienna and report progress. Whoever had fixed the bookings would also have seen that his telephone was wired somewhere in the network outside the hotel. Even using the CC500 would alert them to the fact that he was making contact with the outside world. Yet he must keep Headquarters informed.

From his second briefcase Bond extracted two minute tape recorders, checked the battery strength and set them to voice activation. He rewound both tapes and attached one machine with a sucker microphone the size of a grain of wheat to the telephone. The other he placed in full view, on top of the mini-bar.

Fatigue had caught up with him. He had arranged to meet the others for dinner that evening in the famous snug bar around six. Until then, they had agreed to rest. He rang down for a pot of black coffee and a plate of scrambled eggs. While he waited, Bond examined his room and the small, windowless bathroom. There was a neat shower protected by solidly built sliding glass doors. He approved, and decided to have a shower later. He was hanging his suits in the wardrobe when the waiter arrived with freshly brewed strong coffee and the eggs cooked to perfection.

When he had eaten he placed the ASP near at hand, put the DO

NOT DISTURB sign on the door and settled into one of the comfortable armchairs. Eventually he fell into a deep sleep and dreamed that he was a waiter in a continental café, dashing between the kitchen and the tables as he served M, Tamil Rahani, the now-deceased Poison Dwarf, and Sukie and Nannie. Just before waking he took tea to Sukie and Nannie with a huge cream cake, which disintegrated into sawdust as soon as they tried to cut it. This appeared not to concern either of them, for they paid the bill, each one leaving a piece of jewellery as a tip. He went to pick up a gold bracelet when it slipped, falling with a heavy crash on to a plate.

Bond woke with a start, convinced the noise was real, yet he heard only street noises drifting in through his window. He stretched, uncomfortable and stiff after sleeping in a chair, and glanced at the stainless steel Rolex on his wrist. He was amazed to see that he had slept for several hours. It was almost four-thirty in the afternoon.

Bleary-eyed with sleep, he went to the bathroom, turned on the lights and opened the tall doors to the shower. A strong hot shower followed by an icy one, then a shave and change of clothes would freshen him up.

He began to run the shower, closed the door and started to strip. It crossed his mind that whoever had told him to await orders were taking their time. If he had been manipulating this kidnap, he would have struck almost as soon as his victim had registered at the hotel, getting his quarry out in the open while he was still in bad shape from a night without sleep.

Naked, he went back into the bedroom for the ASP and the baton, which he placed on the floor under a couple of hand towels, just outside the shower. Then he tested the temperature and stepped under the spray. He closed the sliding door and began to soap himself, rubbing his body vigorously with a rough flannel.

Drenched with the hot spray, and exalting in a sense of cleanliness, he altered the settings on the taps, allowing the water to cool quickly until he stood under a shower of almost ice-cold water. The shock hit him, as though he had walked out into a blizzard. Feeling thoroughly revitalised, he turned off the water and shook himself like a dog. Then he reached out to open the sliding door.

Suddenly he was on the alert. He could almost smell danger near by. Before he touched the door handle the lights went out, leaving him disorientated for a second, and in that second he missed the handle, though he heard the door slide open a fraction and close again with a thud. He knew he was now not alone. There was something else in the shower with him, which brushed his face and then went wild, thudding against his body and the sides of the shower.

Bond scrabbled desperately for the door with one hand, flapping the flannel about his face and body with the other to ward off the creature confined with him in the shower. But when his fingers closed over the handle and pulled, the door would not move. The harder he tugged the more vicious the creature's attacks became. He felt a clawing at his shoulder, then his neck, but managed to dislodge it, still hauling on the door, which refused to budge. The thing paused for a moment, as though in preparation for a final assault.

Then he heard Sukie's voice, far away, bright, even flirtatious.

'James? James, where on earth are you?'

'Here! In the bathroom! Get me out, for heaven's sake!'

A second later, the lights went on again. He was aware of Sukie's shadow in the main bathroom. Then he saw his adversary. It was something he had come across only in zoos, and never one as big. Hunched on top of the shower head crouched a giant vampire bat, its evil eyes bright above the razor-toothed mouth, its wings beginning to spread in another attack. He lunged at it with the flannel, shouting,

'Get the shower open!'

The door began to slide open. 'Get out of the bathroom, Sukie. Get out!' Bond wrenched back the door as the bat dived.

He fell sideways into the bathroom, slamming the shower door closed as he did so. He rolled across the floor, making straight for the weapons under the towels.

Although he knew that a vampire bat cannot kill instantly, the thought of what it could inject into his bloodstream was enough to make Bond feel nauseous. And he had not been quick enough, for the creature had escaped with him into the bathroom. He shouted again to Sukie to close the door and wait.

In the space of two heartbeats all he knew of the vampire bat – even its Latin name, the *Desmodus rotundus* – flashed through his mind. There were three varieties. Usually they hunted at night, creeping up on their prey and clamping on to a hairless part of the body with incredibly sharp canine teeth. They sucked blood, at the same time pumping out saliva to stop the blood clotting. It was the saliva that could transmit disease – rabies and other deadly viruses.

This bat was obviously a hybrid and would be carrying some particularly unpleasant disease in its saliva. The lights of the bathroom had completely disorientated it, though it obviously needed blood badly and would fight to sink its teeth into Bond's flesh. Its body was about twenty-seven centimetres long, while the wingspan spread a good sixty centimetres – over three times the length of a normal member of the species.

As though sensing Bond's thoughts, the huge bat raised its front legs, opening the wings to full span and gathered its body up for the fast attack.

Bond's right hand flicked downwards, clicking the baton into its open position. He smashed the weapon hard in the direction of the oncoming creature. His aim succeeded more by luck than judgment, for bats, with their radar-like senses, can usually avoid objects. Probably the unnatural light had something to do with its slow reflexes, for the steel baton caught it directly on the head, throwing it across the room, where it struck the shower doors. With a stride Bond was over the twitching, flapping body and like a man demented he hit the squirming animal again and again. He knew what he was doing, and was aware that fear played no small part in it. As he struck the shattered body time after time his thoughts were of the men who had prepared such a thing as this especially to kill him – for he had little doubt that the saliva of this vampire bat contained something which would bring a fast, painful death.

When he had finished, he dropped the baton in the shower, turned on the spray and walked into the bedroom. He had some disinfectant in the small first aid kit which was now Q Branch standard issue.

He had forgotten about his nakedness.

'Well, now I've seen everything. Quits,' said Sukie, unsmiling, from the chair in which she waited.

There was a small pistol, similar to the one Nannie carried, in her right hand. It was pointing steadily midway between Bond's legs.

10

THE MOZART MAN

Sukie looked hard at Bond, and then down at the gun. 'It's a pretty little thing, isn't it?' She smiled, and he thought he could detect relief in her eyes.

'Just stop pointing it at me. Put on the safety catch and stow it, Sukie.'

She broadened the smile. 'Same goes for you, James.'

Suddenly Bond became aware of his nakedness, and grabbed at the hotel towelling robe as Sukie fitted the small pistol into a holster attached to her white suspender belt.

'Nannie fixed me up with this. Just like hers.' She looked up at him, primly pulling down her skirt. 'I brought your stamps, James. What was going on in the bathroom? For a horrible moment I thought you were having real trouble.'

'I was having trouble, Sukie. Very unpleasant trouble, in the shape of a large hybrid vampire bat, which is not a creature you usually come across in Europe, and especially not in Salzburg. Somebody prepared this one for me.'

'A vam*pire bat*?' Her voice rose in astonishment. 'James! It could have . . .'

'. . . probably killed me. It was almost certainly carrying something even more lethal than rabies or bubonic plague. How did you get in, by the way?'

'I knocked but there was no reply.' She laid the little strip of stamps on the table. 'Then I realised the door was open. It wasn't until I heard the noises coming from the bathroom that I switched on the light. Someone had jammed the shower door with a chair. Actually, I thought it was a practical joke – it's the kind of thing Nannie gets up to – until I heard you shout. I kicked the chair out of the way and moved like lightning.'

'And then waited in here with a loaded gun.'

'Nannie's teaching me to use it. She seems to think it's necessary.'

'And I think it's really necessary for you both to get out of this but thinking won't make it happen. Would you like to do me another favour?'

'Whatever you wish, James.'

Her attitude was suspiciously soft, even yielding. Bond wondered if a girl like Sukie Tempesta would have the guts to handle a dangerous hybrid vampire bat. On balance, he thought, the Principessa Tempesta was perfectly capable of such an act.

'I want you to get me some rubber gloves and a large bottle of antiseptic.'

'Any particular brand?' She stood up.

'Something very strong.'

After Sukie had left on her errand, Bond retrieved the small bottle from the first aid kit and rubbed antiseptic over every inch of his skin. To counteract the strong antiseptic smell he applied cologne. Then he started to dress.

He was concerned about disposing of the bat's corpse. Really it should be incinerated, and the bathroom ought to be fumigated. Bond could hardly go to the hotel manager and explain the circumstances. Plenty of antiseptic, a couple of the hotel plastic carriers and a quick visit to the waste-disposal unit, then hope for the best, he thought.

He put on his grey Cardin suit, a light blue shirt from Hilditch and Key of Jermyn Street, and a white-spotted navy blue tie. The telephone rang and as Bond picked it up he glanced at the tape machine. He saw the tiny cassette begin to turn as he answered curtly.

'Yes.'

'Mr Bond? Is that you, Mr Bond?' It was Kirchtum, breathing heavily and obviously very frightened.

'Yes, Herr Direktor. Are you all right?'

'Physically, yes. They say I am to speak the truth and tell you what a fool I've been.'

'Oh?'

'Yes, I tried to refuse to pass any further instructions to you. I told them they should do this job themselves.'

'And they did not take too kindly to that.' Bond paused, then added for the sake of the tape, 'Particularly as you had already told me I must come with the two ladies to the Goldener Hirsch, here in Salzburg.'

'I must now give you instructions quickly, they say, otherwise they will use the electricity again.' The man sounded on the verge of tears.

'Go ahead. Fast as you like, Herr Doktor.'

Bond knew what Kirchtum was talking about – the brutal, old, but effective method of attaching electrodes to the genitals. Outdated methods of persuasion were often quicker than the drugs used by more sophisticated interrogators nowadays. Kirchtum spoke more rapidly, his voice high-pitched with fear, and Bond could almost see them standing over him, a hand poised on the switch.

'You are to go to Paris tomorrow. It should take you only one day. You must drive on the direct route, and there are rooms booked for you at the George Cinq.'

'Do the ladies have to accompany me?'

'This is essential . . . You understand? Please say you understand, Mr Bond . . .'

'I . . .' He was interrupted by an hysterical scream. Had the switch been pulled for encouragement? 'I understand.'

'Good.' It was not the doctor speaking now, but a hollow, distorted voice. 'Good. Then you will save the two ladies we are holding from a most unpleasant, slow end. We shall speak again in Paris, Bond.'

The line went dead, and Bond picked up the miniature tape machine. He ran the tape back and replayed it through its tiny speaker. At least he could get this information to Vienna or London. The final echoing voice on the line might also be of some small help to them. Even if the men terrorising Kirchtum at the Klinik Mozart had used an electronic 'voice handkerchief', there was still the chance that Q Branch might take an accurate voice print from it. At least if they could make some identification, M would know which particular organisation Bond was dealing with.

He went over to the desk and removed the tiny cassette from the tape machine, nipping off the little plastic safety lug to prevent the tape from being accidentally recorded over. He addressed a stout envelope in M's cover name as Chairman of Transworld, at one of the safe Post Office box numbers, folded the cassette into a sheet of hotel writing paper, on which he had written a few words, and sealed the envelope. Guessing the weight of the package, he added stamps.

He had just finished this important chore when a knock at the door heralded Sukie's return. She carried a brown paper sack containing her purchases, and appeared inclined to stay in the room until Bond firmly suggested that she join Nannie and wait in the snug bar for him.

The job of cleaning up the bathroom, wearing the rubber gloves and using almost the entire bottle of antiseptic which Sukie had brought him took fifteen minutes. Before completing the job he added the gloves to the neat, sinister parcel containing the remains of the vampire bat. He was as sure as he could be that no germs had entered his system.

While he worked, Bond thought of the possibilities regarding the perpetrator of this last attempt on his life. He was almost certain that it was his old enemy, SMERSH – now Directorate S's Department Eight of the KGB – who were holding Kirchtum, and using him as their personal messenger. But was it really their style to use such a thing as a hybrid vampire bat against him?

Who, he wondered, would have the resources to work on the breeding and development of a weapon so horrible? It struck him that the creature must have taken a number of years to be brought to its present state, and that indicated a large organisation, with funds and the specialist expertise required. The work would have been carried out in a simulated warm forest-like environment, for, if his memory was correct, the species' natural habitats were the jungles and forests of Mexico, Chile, Argentina and Uruguay.

Money, special facilities, time and zoologists without scruples: SPECTRE was the obvious bet, though any well-funded outfit with an interest in terrorism and killings would be on the list, for the creature would not have been developed simply as a one-off to inject some terrible terminal disease into Bond's bloodstream. The Bulgarians and Czechs favoured that kind of thing, and he would not even put it past Cuba to send some agent of their well-trained internal G-2 out into the wider field of international intrigue. The Honoured Society, that polite term for the Mafia, was also a possibility – for they were not beyond selling the goods to terrorist organisations, as long as they were not used within the borders of the United States, Sicily or Italy.

But, when the chips were down, Bond plumped for SPECTRE itself – only, once more during this strange dance with death, someone had saved him, at the last moment, from another attempted execution, and this time it was Sukie, a young woman met seemingly by accident. Could she be the truly dangerous one?

He sought out the kitchens and with a great deal of charm explained that some food had been left accidentally in his car. He asked if there was an incinerator and a porter man was summoned to lead him to it. The man even offered to dispose of the bundle himself, but Bond tipped him heavily and said he would like to see it burned.

It was already six-twenty. Before going to the bar he made a last visit to his room and doused himself in cologne to disguise any remaining traces of the antiseptic.

Sukie and Nannie were anxious to hear what he had been doing, but Bond merely said they would be told all in good time. For the moment they should enjoy the pleasanter things of life. After a drink in the snug bar, they moved to the table which Nannie had been sensible enough to reserve and dined on the famous Viennese boiled beef dish called *Tafelspitz*. It was like no other boiled beef on earth, a gastronomic delight, with a piquant vegetable sauce, and served with melting sautéed potatoes. They had resisted a first course for it is sacrilege to decline dessert in an Austrian restaurant. They chose the light, fragile *Salzburger soufflé*, said to have been created nearly three hundred years ago by a chef in the Hohensalzburg. It arrived topped by a mountain of *Schlag*, rich whipped cream.

Afterwards they went outside among the strolling window-shoppers in the warm air of the Getreidegasse. Bond wanted to be safe from bugging equipment.

'I'm too full,' said Nannie, hobbling with one hand on her stomach.

'You're going to need the food with what the night has in store for us,' Bond said quietly.

'Promises, promises,' Sukie muttered, breathing heavily. 'I feel like a dirigible. So what's in store, James?'

He told them they would be driving to Paris.

'You've made it plain that you're coming with me, whatever. The people who are giving me the run-around have also insisted that you're to accompany me, and I have to be sure that you do. The lives of a very dear friend, and an equally dear colleague are genuinely at risk. I can say no more.'

'Of course we're coming,' Sukie snapped.

'Try and stop us,' added Nannie.

'I'm going to do one thing out of line,' he explained. 'The orders are that we start tomorrow – which means they expect us to do it in daylight. I'm starting shortly after midnight. That way

I can plead that we did start the drive tomorrow, but we might get a jump ahead of them. It's not much, but it may just throw them off balance.'

It was agreed that they would meet by the car on the stroke of midnight. As they started to retrace their steps towards the Goldener Hirsch, Bond paused briefly by a letter box set into the wall and slid his package from his breast pocket to the box. It was neatly done, in seconds, and he was fairly certain that even Sukie and Nannie did not notice.

It was just after ten when he got back to his room. By ten-thirty the briefcases and his bag were packed, and he had changed into casual jeans and jacket. He was carrying the ASP and the baton as usual. With an hour and a half to go, Bond sat down and concentrated on how he might gain the initiative in this wild and dangerous death hunt.

So far, the attempts on his life had been cunning. Only in their early encounters had someone else stepped in to save his life, presumably in order to set him up for the final act in the drama. He knew that he could trust nobody – especially Sukie since she had revealed herself as his saviour, however unwitting, in the vampire bat incident. But how could he now take some command over the situation? Suddenly he thought of Kirchtum, held prisoner in his own clinic. The last thing they would expect would be an assault on this power base. It was a fifteen minute drive out of Salzburg to the Klinik Mozart and time was short. If he could find the right car, perhaps it was just possible.

Bond left the room and hurried downstairs to the reception desk to ask what self-drive hire cars were immediately available. For once, he seemed to be making his own luck. There was a Saab 900 Turbo, a car he knew well, which had only just been returned. A couple of short telephone calls secured it for him. It was waiting only four minutes' walk from the hotel.

As he waited for the cashier to take his credit card details, he walked over to the internal telephones and rang Nannie's number. She answered immediately.

'Say nothing,' he said quietly. 'Wait in your room. I may have to delay departure for an hour. Tell Sukie.'

She agreed, but sounded surprised. By the time he returned to the desk, the formalities had been completed.

Five minutes later, having collected the car from a smiling representative, Bond was driving skilfully out of Salzburg on the mountain road to the south, passing in the suburbs the strange Anif water-tower which rises like an English manor house from the middle of a pond. He continued almost as far as the town of Hallein, which had begun as an island bastion in the middle of the Salzach and which has been made famous as the birthplace of Franz-Xavier Gruber, the composer of *Stille Nacht, Heilige Nacht.*

The Klinik Mozart stands back from the road, about two kilometres on the Salzburg side of Hallein, the seventeenth-century house screened from passing view by woods.

Bond pulled the Saab into a lay-by. He switched off the headlights and the engine, put on the reverse lock and climbed out. A few moments later he had ducked under the wooden fencing and was moving carefully through the trees, peering in the darkness for his first sight of the clinic. He had no idea how the security of the clinic was arranged; neither did he know how many people he was up against.

He reached the edge of the trees just as the moon came out. There was light streaming from many of the large windows at the front of the building, but the grounds were in darkness. As his eyes adjusted, Bond tried to pick up movement across the hundred metres of open space that separated him from the house. There were four cars parked on the wide gravel drive but no sign of life. Gently he eased out the ASP, gripping it in his right hand. He took the baton in his left and flicked it open, ready for use. Then he broke cover, moving fast and silently, remaining on the grass and avoiding the long drive up to the house.

Nothing moved and there was not a sound. He reached the gravel forecourt and tried to remember where the Direktor's office was situated in relation to the front door. Somewhere to the right, he thought, remembering how he had stood at the tall windows when he had come to arrange May's admission, looking out at the lawns and the drive. Now he had a fix, for he recalled that they were French windows. There were French windows immediately to his right showing chinks of light through the closed curtains.

He eased himself towards the windows, realising with thudding heart that they were open and muffled voices could be heard from inside. He was close enough actually to hear, if he concentrated, what was being said.

'You cannot keep me here for ever – not with only three of you.' It was the Direktor's voice that he recognised first. The bluffness had disappeared, and was replaced by a pleading tone. 'Surely you've done enough.'

'We've managed well enough so far,' another voice said. 'You have been co-operative – to a point – Herr Direktor, but we cannot take chances. We shall leave only when Bond is secure and our people are far away. The situation is ideal for the short-wave transmitter; and your patients have not suffered. Another twenty-four, maybe forty-eight hours will make little difference to you. Eventually we shall leave you in peace.'

'*Stille Nacht, Heilige Nacht,*' a third voice chanted with a chuckle. Bond's blood ran cold. He moved closer to the windows, the tips of his fingers resting against the open crack.

'You wouldn't . . .' There was trembling terror in Kirchturn's voice, not hysterical fear, but the genuine terror that strikes a man facing death by torture.

'You've seen our faces, Herr Direktor. You know who we are.'

'I would never . . .'

'Don't even think about it. You have one more message to pass for us when Bond gets to Paris. After that . . . Well, we shall see.'

Bond shivered. He had recognised a voice he would never have thought, in a thousand years, he would hear in this situation. He took a deep breath and slowly pulled, widening the crack between the windows. Then he moved the curtains a fraction to peer into the room.

Kirchtum was strapped into an old-fashioned desk chair with a circular seat, made of wood and leather, and with three legs on castors. The bookcase behind him had been swept clean and books replaced by a powerful radio transmitter. A broad-shouldered man sat in front of the radio, another stood behind Kirchtum's chair, and the third, legs apart, faced the Direktor. Bond recognised him at once, just as he had known the voice.

He breathed in through his nose, lifted the ASP and lunged through the windows. There was no time for hesitation. What he had heard told him that the three men constituted the entire enemy force at the Klinik Mozart.

The ASP thumped four times, two bullets shattering the chest of the man behind Kirchtum's chair, the other two plunging into the back of the radio operator. The third man whirled around, mouth open, hand moving to his hip.

'Hold it there, Quinn! One move and your legs go – right?'

Steve Quinn, the Service's man in Rome, stood rock still, his mouth curving into a snarl as Bond removed the pistol from inside his jacket.

'Mr Bond? How . . . ?' Kirchtum spoke in a hoarse whisper.

'You're finished, James. No matter what you do to me, you're finished.' Quinn had not quite regained his composure, but he made a good attempt.

'Not quite,' said Bond smiling, but without triumph. 'Not quite yet, though I admit I was surprised to find you here. Who are you really working for, Quinn? SPECTRE?'

'No.' Quinn gave him the shadow of a smile. 'Pure KGB First Chief Directorate, naturally – for years, and not even Tabby knows. Now on temporary detachment to Department Eight, your old sparring partner, SMERSH. Unlike you, James, I've always been a Mozart man. I prefer to dance to good music.'

'Oh, you'll dance.' Bond's expression betrayed the cold, cruel streak that was the darkest side of his nature.

11

HAWK'S WING AND MACABRE

James Bond was not prepared to waste time. He knew, to his cost, the dangers of keeping an enemy talking. It was a technique he had used to his own advantage before now, and Steve Quinn was quite capable of trying to play for time. Crisply, still keeping his distance, Bond ordered him to stand well away from the wall, spread his legs, stretch out his arms and lean forward, palms against the wall. Once in that position, he made Quinn shuffle his feet back even further so that he had no leverage for a quick attack.

Only then did Bond approach Quinn and frisk him with great care. There was a small Smith & Wesson Chief's Special revolver tucked into the waistband of his trousers, at the small of his back. A tiny automatic pistol, an Austrian Steyr 6.35 mm was taped to the inside of his left calf, and a wicked little flick knife to the outside of his right ankle.

'Haven't seen one of these in years,' said Bond as he tossed the Steyr on to the desk. 'No grenades secreted up your backside, I trust.' He did not smile. 'You're a damned walking arsenal, man. You should be careful. Terrorists might be tempted to break into you.'

'In this game, I've always found it useful to keep a few tricks up my sleeve.'

As he spoke the last word, Steve Quinn let his body sag. He collapsed on to the floor and in the fraction of a second flip-rolled to the right, his arm reaching towards the table where the Steyr automatic lay.

'Don't try it!' Bond snapped, taking aim with the ASP.

Quinn was not ready to die for the cause for which he had betrayed the Service. He froze, his hand still raised, like an overgrown child playing the old game of statues.

'Face down! Spreadeagled!' Bond ordered, looking around the room for something to secure his prisoner. Keeping the ASP levelled at Quinn, he sidled behind Kirchtum, and used his left hand to unbuckle the two short and two long straps obviously designed to restrain violent patients. As he moved he continued to snap orders at Quinn.

'Face right down, eat the carpet, you bastard, and get your legs wider apart, arms in the crucifix position.'

Quinn obeyed, grunting obscenities. As the last buckle gave way, Kirchtum began to rub the circulation back into his arms and legs. His wrists were marked where the hard leather thongs had bitten into his flesh.

'Stay seated,' Bond whispered. 'Don't move. Give the circulation a chance.'

Taking the straps, he approached Quinn with his gun hand well back, knowing that a lashing foot could catch his wrist.

'The slightest move and I'll blow a hole in you so big that even the maggots will need maps. Understand?'

Quinn grunted and Bond kicked his legs together, viciously hitting his ankle with the steel-capped toe of his shoe so that he yelped with pain. While the agony was sweeping through him, Bond swiftly slid one of the straps around Quinn's ankles, pulled hard and buckled the leather tightly.

'Now the arms! Fingers laced behind your back!'

As though to make him understand, Bond knocked the right wrist with his foot. There was another cry of pain, but Quinn obeyed, and Bond secured his wrists with another strap.

'This may be old-fashioned, but it'll keep you quiet until we've made more permanent arrangements,' Bond muttered as he buckled the two long straps together. He fastened one end of the elongated strap around Quinn's ankles, then brought the rest up around his neck and back to the ankles. He pulled tightly, bringing the prisoner's head up and forcing the legs towards his trunk. Indeed it was a method old and well tried. If the captive struggled he would strangle himself, for the straps were pulled so tightly that they made Quinn's body into a bow, with the feet and neck as the outer edges. Even if he tried to relax his legs, the strap would pull hard on the neck.

Quinn let out a stream of obscene abuse, and Bond, enraged now at discovering an old friend to be a mole, kicked him hard in the ribs. He took out a handkerchief and stuffed it into Quinn's mouth with a curt, 'Shut up!'

For the first time Bond had a real chance to look around the room. It was furnished in solid nineteenth-century style – a heavy desk, the bookcases rising to the ceiling, the chairs with curved backs. Kirchtum still sat at the desk, his face pale, hands shaking. The big, expansive man had turned to terrified blubber.

Bond went over to the radio, stepping over the books that had been swept off the shelves. The radio operator was slumped in his chair, the blood dripping on to the carpet bright against the faded pattern. Bond pushed the body unceremoniously from the chair. He did not recognise the face, twisted in the surprised agony of death. The other corpse lay sprawled against the wall, as though he was a drunk collapsed at a party. Bond could not put a name to him, but had seen the photograph in the files – East German, a criminal with terrorist leanings. It was amazing, he thought, how many of Europe's violent villains were turning into mercenaries for the terrorist organisations. Rent-a-Thug, he thought, as he turned to Kirchtum.

'How did they manage it?' he asked blandly, seemingly drained by the knowledge that Quinn had sold out.

'Manage?' Kirchtum appeared to be at a loss.

'Look – ' Bond almost shouted before realising that Kirchturn's English was not always perfect, and could have deserted him in his present state. He walked over and laid an arm on the man's shoulder, speaking quietly and sympathetically. 'Look, Herr Doktor, I need information from you very quickly, especially if we are ever to see the two ladies alive again.'

'Oh, my God.' Kirchtum covered his face with his big, thick hands. 'It is my fault that Miss May and her friend . . . Never should I have allowed Miss May to go out.' He was near to tears.

'No. No, not your fault. How were you to know? Just calm yourself and answer my questions as carefully as you can. How did these men manage to get in and hold you here?'

Kirchtum let his fingers slide down his face. His eyes were full of desolation. 'Those . . . those two . . .' He gestured at the bodies. 'They came as repair men for the *Antenne* – what you call it? The pole? For the television . . .'

'The television aerial.'

'*Ja*, the television aerial. The duty nurse let them in, and on to the roof. She thought it good, okay. Only when she was coming to me did I smell a mouse.'

'They asked to see you?'

'In here. My office, they ask. Only later I find they had been putting up *Antenne* for their radio equipment. They lock the door. They threaten me with guns and torture. Tell me to put the next doctor in charge of the clinic. To say I would be occupied in my study on business matters for a day or two. They laughed when I had to say "tied up". They had pistols. Guns. What could I do?'

'You do not argue with loaded guns,' Bond agreed, 'as you can see.' He nodded to the corpses. Then he turned to the grunting, straining Steve Qumn. 'And when did this piece of scum arrive?'

'The same night, later. Through the windows, like you.'

'Which night was that?'

'The day after the ladies disappeared. The two in the afternoon, the other at night. By that time they had me in this chair. All the time they had me here, except when I had to perform functions . . .' Bond looked surprised, and Kirchturn said he meant natural functions. 'Finally I refused to give you messages on the telephone. Until then they had only threatened me. But after that . . .'

Bond had already seen the bowl of water and the large crocodile clips wired up to a socket in the wall. He nodded, knowing only too well what Kirchtum must have suffered.

'And the radio?' he asked.

'Ah, yes. They used it quite often. Twice, three times a day.'

'Did you hear anything?' Bond looked at the radio. There were two sets of earphones jacked into the receiver.

'Most of it. They wear the earphones sometimes, but there are speakers there, see.'

Indeed, there were two small circular speakers set into the centre of the system. 'Tell me what you heard.'

'What to tell? They spoke. Another man spoke from far away . . .'

'Who spoke first? Did the other man call them?'

Kirchtum thought for a moment. 'Ah, yes. The voice would come with a lot of crackling.'

Bond, standing beside the sophisticated high frequency transmitter, saw that the dials were glowing and heard a faint hum from the speakers. He noted the dial settings. They had been talking to someone a long way off – anything from six hundred to six thousand kilometres away.

'Can you remember if the messages came at any specific times?'

Kirchtum's brow creased, and then he nodded. 'Ja. Yes, I think so. In the mornings. Early. Six o'clock. Then at midday . . .'

'Six in the evening and again at midnight?'

'Something like that, yes. But not quite.'

'Just before the hour, or just after, yes?'

'That is right.'

'Anything else?'

The doctor paused, thought again, and then nodded. 'Ja. I

know they have to send a message when news comes that you are leaving Salzburg. They have a man watching . . .'

'The hotel?'

'No. I heard the talk. He is watching the road. He is to telephone when you drive away and they have to make a signal with the radio. They must use special words . . .'

'Can you remember them?'

'Something like the package is posted to Paris.'

That sounded par for the course, Bond thought. Cloak and dagger. The Russians, like the Nazis before them, read too many bad espionage novels.

'Were there any other special words?'

'Yes, they used others. The man at the other end calls himself Hawk's Wing – I thought it strange.'

'And here?'

'Here they call themselves Macabre.'

'So, when the radio comes on, the other end says something like, "Macabre this is Hawk's Wing . . ." '

'Over.'

'Over, yes. And, "Come in Hawk's Wing." '

'This is just how they say it, yes.'

'Why haven't any of your staff come to this office, or alerted the police? There must have been noise. I have used a gun.'

Kirchtum shrugged. 'The noise of your gun might have been heard from the windows, but the windows only. My office is soundproofed because sometimes there are disturbing noises from the clinic. This is why they opened the windows here. They opened them a few times a day for the circulation of air. It can get most heavy in here with the soundproofing. Even the windows are soundproofed with the double glaze.'

Bond nodded and glanced at his watch. It was almost eleven forty-five. Hawk's Wing would be making his call at any time, and he had already figured that Quinn's man would be stationed somewhere near the E11 autobahn. In fact he probably had all exit roads watched. Nice and professional. Far better than just one man at the hotel.

But he was now playing for time. Quinn had stopped twisting on the floor, and Bond was already beginning to work out a scheme that would take care of him. The man had been in the game a long time, and his experience and training would make him hard to crack, even under ideal interrogation conditions; violence would be counter-productive. There was, he knew, only one way to get at Stephen Quinn.

He went over and knelt beside the trussed figure. 'Quinn,' he said softly, and saw the hate in the sidelong, painful glance. 'We need your co-operation.'

Quinn grunted through the makeshift gag. It was clear that in no way would Quinn co-operate.

'I know the telephone is insecure, but I'm calling Vienna for a relay to London. I want you to listen very carefully.'

He went over to the desk, lifted the receiver and dialled 0222–43–16–08, the Tourist Board offices in Vienna, where he knew there would be an answering machine at this time of night. He held the receiver away from his ear so that Quinn would at least hear a muffled answer. When it came, Bond put the receiver very close to his ear, simultaneously pressing the rest button.

'Predator,' he said softly. Then, after a pause, 'Yes. Priority for London to copy and action soonest. Rome's gone off the rails.' He paused again, as though listening. 'Yes, working for Centre. I have him, but we need more. I want a snatch team at Flat 28, 48 Via Barberini – it's next to the JAL offices. Lift Tabitha Quinn and hold for orders. Tell them to alert Hereford and call in one of the psychos if M doesn't want dirty hands.'

Behind him, he heard Quinn grunting, getting agitated. A threat to his wife was the only thing that would have any effect.

'That's right. Will do. I'll run it through you, but termination, or near termination may be necessary. I'll get back within the hour. Good.' He put down the instrument. When he knelt again

beside Quinn, the look in the man's eyes had changed; hatred
was now edged with anxiety.

'It's okay, Steve. Nobody's going to hurt you. But, I'm afraid it
could be different with Tabby. I'm sorry.'

There was no way that Quinn could even suspect a bluff, or
double bluff. He had been in the Service for a long time himself,
and was well aware that calling in a psycho – the Service name
for their mercenary killers – was no idle threat. He knew the
many ways his wife could suffer before she died. He had worked
with Bond for years and was sure 007 would show no compunc-
tion in carrying out the threat.

Bond continued, 'I gather there will be a call coming through
I'm going to strap you into the chair in front of the radio. Make
the responses fast. Get off the air quickly. Feign bad transmission
if you have to. But, Steve, don't do anything out of line – no
missing out words or putting in "alert" sentences. I'll be able
to tell, as you know. Just as you'd be able to detect a dodgy
response. If you do make a wrong move, you'll wake up in
Warminster to a long interrogation and a longer time in jail.
You'll also be shown photographs of what they did to Tabby
before she died. That I promise you. Now . . .'

He manhandled Quinn into the radio operator's chair, and
adjusted the straps from the strangulation position, binding him
tightly into the chair. He felt confident, for the fight appeared
to have gone out of Steve Quinn. But you could never tell. The
defector might well be so indoctrinated that he could bring
himself to sacrifice his wife.

At last he asked if Quinn was willing to play it straight. The big
man just nodded his head sullenly, and Bond pulled the gag
from his mouth.

'You bastard!' Quinn said in a hoarse, breathless voice.

'It can happen to the best of us, Steve. Just do as you're told
and there's a chance that both of you will live.'

As he was speaking, the transmitter hummed and crackled

into life. Bond's hand went out to the receive and send switch, set to Receive. A disembodied voice recited the code:

'Hawk's Wing to Macabre. Hawk's Wing to Macabre. Come in Macabre.'

Bond nodded to Quinn, clicked the switch to Send, and for the first time in years prayed.

12

ENGLAND EXPECTS

'Macabre, Hawk's Wing, I have you. Over.'

Steve Quinn's voice sounded too steady for Bond's liking, but he had to let him go through with it. The voice at the distant end crackled through the small speakers.

'Hawk's Wing, Macabre, routine check. Report situation. Over.'

Quinn paused for a second, and Bond allowed the muzzle of the ASP to touch him behind the ear.

'Situation normal. We await developments. Over.'

'Call back when package is on its way. Over.'

'Wilco, Hawk's Wing. Over and out.'

There was silence for a moment as the switch was clicked to the Receive position again. Then Bond turned to Kirchtum, asking if it all sounded normal.

'It was usual,' he said with a nod.

'Right, Herr Doktor. Now you come into your own. Can you get something that will put this bastard to sleep for around four or five hours, and make him wake up feeling reasonable – no slurred speech or anything?'

'I have just the thing.'

For the first time, Kirchtum smiled, easing his body painfully from the chair and hobbling towards the door. Half-way there he realised that he was wearing no shoes or socks and limped back to retrieve them. He put them on and slowly left the room.

'If you have by any chance alerted Hawk's Wing, you know

that Tabby won't last long once we've found you out. You do everything by the book, Quinn, and I'll do my best for you as well. But the first person to be concerned about is your wife. Right?'

Quinn glared at him with the hatred of a traitor who knows he's cornered.

'This applies to your information as well. I want straight answers, and I want them now.'

'I might not have the answers.'

'You just tell me what you know. We'll know truth from fiction in the long run.'

Quinn did not reply.

'First, what's going to happen in Paris? At the George Cinq?'

'Our people are going for you. At the hotel.'

'But you could have got me here. Enough people have tried already.'

'Not my people. Not KGB. We banked on you coming down here after May and Moneypenny. Yes, we organised the kidnap. The idea was for us to take you on from here. Getting you to Salzburg was like putting you into a funnel.'

'Then it wasn't your people who had a go in the car?'

'No. One of the competition. They took out the Service people. None of my doing. You seem to have had a guardian angel all the way. The two men I put on to you were from the Rome Station. I was to burn them once they saw you safely into Salzburg.'

'And send me on to Paris?'

'Yes, blast you. If it were anyone else but Tabby, I'd . . .'

'But it is Tabby we're thinking about.' Bond paused. 'Paris? Why Paris?'

Quinn stared steadily into Bond's eyes. The man did know something more. 'Why Paris? Remember Tabby.'

'The rules are it's to be Berlin, Paris or London. They want your head, Bond, but they want to see it done. We were out to claim the reward and just taking your head wasn't enough. My instructions were to get you to Paris. The people there have orders to pick you up, and . . .'

He stopped, as though he'd already said enough.

'And deliver the package?'

There was fifteen seconds' silence.

'Yes.'

'Deliver it where?'

'To the Man.'

'Tamil Rahani? The head of SPECTRE?'

'Yes.'

'Deliver it where?' Bond repeated.

No response.

'Remember Tabby, Quinn. I'll see Tabby suffers great pain before she dies. Then they'll come for you. Where am I to be delivered?'

The silence stretched for what seemed to be minutes.

'Florida.'

'Where in Florida? Big place, Florida. Where? Disney World?'

Quinn looked away. 'The most southern tip of the United States,' he said.

'Ah.' Bond nodded.

The Florida Keys, he thought. Those linked islands that stretch 150 kilometres out into the ocean. Bahai Honda Key, Big Pine Key, Cudjoe Key, Boca Chica Key – the names of the most famous ones flicked through his mind. But, the southernmost tip – well, that was Key West, once the home of Ernest Hemingway, a narcotics route, a tourist paradise, with a sprinkling of islands outside the reef. Ideal, thought Bond. Key West – who would have imagined SPECTRE setting up its headquarters there?

'Key West,' he said aloud, and Quinn gave a small, ashamed nod. 'Paris, London or Berlin. They could have included Rome and other major cities. Anywhere they could get me on to a direct Miami flight, eh?'

'I suppose so.'

'Where exactly in Key West?'

'That I don't know. Honestly, I just do not know.'

Bond shrugged as though to say it did not matter.

The door opened and Kirchtum came in. He was smiling as he flourished a kidney bowl covered with a cloth.

'I have what you need, I think.'

'Good,' said Bond, smiling back, 'and I think I have what I need. Put him out, Herr Doktor.'

Quinn did not resist as Kirchtum rolled up his sleeve, swabbed a patch on the upper right arm and slid the hypodermic needle in. It took less than ten seconds for his body to relax and the head to loll over. Bond was already busy with the straps again.

'He will have a good four to five hours' sleeping. You are leaving?'

'Yes, when I've made sure he can't get away once he wakes up. One of my people should arrive here before then, to see that he gets the telephone call from his watcher and relays it on to his source. I have to arrange that. My man will use the words, "Ill met by moonlight." You reply, "Proud Titania." Got it?'

'This is Shakespeare, the *Summer Midnight Dream, ja*?'

'*A Midsummer Night's Dream, ja*, Herr Doktor.'

'So, summer midnight, midsummer night's, what's the difference?'

'It obviously mattered to Mr Shakespeare. Better get it right.' Bond smiled at the bear-like doctor. 'Can you deal with all this?'

'Try me, Herr Bond.'

Five minutes later, Bond was heading back to the Saab. He drove fast to the hotel. In his room he called Nannie to apologise for keeping them waiting.

'There's been a slight change of plan,' he told her. 'Just stand by. Tell Sukie. I'll be in touch soon. With luck, we'll be leaving within the hour.'

'What the hell's going on?' Nannie sounded peeved.

'Just stay put. Don't worry, I won't leave without you.'

'I should jolly well think not,' she snapped, banging down the receiver.

Bond smiled to himself, opened up the briefcase containing the CC500 scrambler and attached it to the telephone. Though he was, to all intents and purposes, on his own, it was time to call for some limited assistance from the Service.

He dialled the London Regent's Park number, knowing the line would be safe now he had taken out the team at the clinic, and asked for the Duty Officer who came on almost immediately. After identifying himself, Bond began to issue his instructions. There was information he wanted relayed fast to M, and on to the Vienna Resident. He was precise and firm, saying that there was only one way to deal with the matter – his way. Otherwise they could lose the chance of a lifetime. SPECTRE had made themselves into a sitting target, which only he could smash. His instructions had to be carried out to the letter. He ended by repeating the hotel number and his room and asked for a call-back as quickly as possible.

It took just over fifteen minutes. M had okayed all Bond's instructions and the operation was already running from Vienna. A private jet would bring in a team of five – three men and two women. They would wait at Salzburg airport for Bond who should get clearance for a private flight to Zurich on his Universal Export passport B. Bookings were made on the Pan American Flight 115 from Zurich to Miami, departing at 10.15 local time. Bond thanked the Duty Officer and was about to close the line when he was stopped.

'Predator.'

'Yes?'

'Private message from M.'

'Go on.'

'He says, "England expects". Nelson, I suppose – "England expects that every man will do his duty." '

'Yes,' Bond replied irritably. 'I do know the quotation.'

'And he says good luck, sir.'

He knew he would need every ounce of luck that came his way. He unhooked the CC500 and dialled Nannie's room.

'All set. We're almost ready for the off.'

'About time. Where are we going?'

'Off to see the Wizard.' Bond laughed without humour. 'The Wonderful Wizard of Oz.'

13

GOOD EVENING, MR BOLDMAN

'James. James, you're going the wrong way. You left the Bentley in the car park to the left. Remember?'

'Don't tell the whole world, Sukie. We're not using the Bentley.'

On his way back, after parking the Saab, he had made a quick detour, and used the old trick of sticking the Bentley's keys up the exhaust pipe. It was not as safe as he would have liked, but it would have to do. Now they were lugging their suitcases to the Saab.

'Not . . .' There was an intake of breath from Nannie.

'We have alternative transport,' Bond said crisply, his voice sharp with authority.

His plan to outflank SPECTRE depended entirely on caution and timing. He had even considered ditching Sukie and Nannie, leaving them in the hotel. But, unless he could isolate them, it was a safer course to take them along. They had already shown their determination to remain with him anyway. Dumping them now was asking for trouble.

'I hope your American visas are up to date,' Bond said, once they had packed everything into the car and he had started the engine.

'American?' Sukie's voice rose in a petulant squeak.

'Visas not okay?'

He edged out of the parking place and began to negotiate the streets that would take them on to the airport road.

'Of course they are!' Nannie sounded cross.

'I haven't a thing to wear,' Sukie said loudly.

'Jeans and a shirt will do where we're going.'

Bond smiled as he turned on to the Innsbruck road. The *Flughafen* sign was illuminated for a second in his headlights.

'Another thing,' he added. 'Before we leave this car you'll have to stow your hardware in one of my cases. We're heading for Zurich, then flying direct to the States. I have a shielded compartment in my big case and our weapons will have to go in there. From Zurich we'll be on commercial airlines.'

Nannie began to protest and Bond quickly cut her short. 'You both decided to stay with me on this. If you want out, then say so now and I'll have you taken back to the hotel. You can have fun going to all those Mozart concerts.'

'We're coming, whatever,' Nannie said firmly. 'Both of us. Okay, Sukie?'

'You bet your sweet . . .'

'As arranged, then.' Bond could see the *Flughafen* signs coming up fast now. 'There's a private jet on its way for us. I shall have to spend some time with the people who will be arriving on it. You cannot be in on that, I'm afraid. Then we take off for Zurich.'

In the airport car park, Bond opened up the hatchback and unzipped his folding Samsonite case. Q Branch had taken it apart and fitted a sturdy extra zipped compartment in the centre. This was impervious to all airport surveillance and Bond had found it invaluable when travelling with airlines not allowing him to carry a personal weapon.

'Anything you should not be carrying, ladies, please.'

He held out a hand while both Sukie and Nannie hoisted their skirts and unclipped from their suspender belts the identical holsters carrying automatic pistols. When the case had been returned to the luggage compartment, he ushered them back into the car.

'Remember, you're unarmed. But as far as I can tell, there's no danger. The people who are on my trail should have been diverted. I shall be with the airport manager.'

He told them he would not be long, and then walked towards the airport buildings. The airport manager had been alerted and was treating the arrival of the executive aircraft as a normal routine matter.

'They are about eighty kilometres out, and just starting their approach,' he told Bond. 'I believe you need a room for a small conference while the aircraft is being turned around.'

Bond nodded, apologising for the inconvenience of having the airport opened at this time of night.

'Just be grateful the weather is good,' the manager said with an uncertain smile. 'It's not possible at night if there is a lot of cloud.'

They went out on to the apron, and Bond saw that the airport had been lit for the arrival. A few minutes later he spotted the flashing red and green lights creeping down the invisible path of the approach to the main runway. In a few seconds the little HS 125 Exec jet, bearing no markings but a British identification number, came hissing in over the threshold. It touched down neatly and pulled up with a sharp deceleration. The pilot had obviously used Salzburg before and knew its limits. The aircraft was brought to a standstill by a 'batsman' using a pair of illuminated batons.

The forward door opened and the gangway was unfolded. Bond did not recognise the two women, but was glad to see that at least two of the men coming down the steps were people he had worked with before. The more senior was a bronzed, athletic young man called Crispin Thrush, with Service experience almost as varied as Bond's.

The two men shook hands, and Crispin introduced him to the other members of the team as the manager led them to a small, deserted conference room. Coffee, bottles of mineral water, and note pads were set out on a circular table.

'Help yourselves,' Bond said as he looked around at the team.

'I think I'll go and wash my hands.' He jerked his head at Crispin, who nodded and followed him from the room out into the airport car park. They spoke in lowered voices.

'They briefed you?' Bond asked.

'Only the basics. Said you'd put the flesh on it.'

'Right. You and one of the other chaps take a rented Saab – the one with the two girls in it, over there – and go straight up to the Klinik Mozart. You've got the route?'

Thrush nodded. 'Yes, they gave us that. And I was told something almost unbelievable . . .'

'Steve?'

He nodded again.

'Well, it's true. You'll find him there, sleeping off some dope the clinic's Director, Doktor Kirchtum, gave him. You'll find Kirchtum a godsend. Quinn and a couple of heavies have been holding him there.'

He went on to explain that there was some cleaning up to be done, and Quinn was to be made ready to take a telephone call from the KGB man watching the road for the Bentley. 'When he makes his radio report, listen to him and watch him, Crispin. He's a rogue agent, and I've no need to tell you how dangerous that can be. He knows all the tricks and I've only got his co-operation because of threats against his wife . . .'

'They pulled Tabby in, I understand. She's stashed in one of the Rome safe houses. Gather the poor girl's a bit confused.'

'Probably doesn't believe it. He says she had no idea that he'd defected. Anyway, if the whole team will fit into the Saab, you'd better drop your two girls, and the other lad off at the Goldener Hirsch. If we keep it short in the conference room, you can get the Bentley team on their way. The car will be spotted, so make sure you've got time to get settled into the clinic, with Quinn awake, before the Bentley leaves. Their watcher will take it for granted that I'm in it, with my companions, heading for Paris. That should throw them for a while.'

He told Crispin where the Bentley could be found, with the

keys in the exhaust, and the route the team should take to Paris. Once the messages had been passed on, Crispin and his man were to get Steve Quinn to Vienna by the fastest means possible.

'Tickets. With the Resident's compliments.'

Crispin reached into his jacket and pulled out a heavy, long envelope. Bond slid it unopened into his breast pocket, as they began walking slowly back to the conference room. They stayed there for less than fifteen minutes, drinking coffee and improvising a business meeting concerning an export deal in chocolate. Eventually Bond rose.

'Right, ladies and gentlemen. See you outside, then.'

He had already arranged that Sukie and Nannie would not even see the team that had flown in. He used some charm to get a man to remove their luggage from the Saab, and now he briskly ushered them into the airport building, where the manager was waiting for them. He joined them a few minutes later, having passed on the Saab keys to Crispin, and wished the new team good luck.

'M's going to boil you in oil if this goes wrong,' Crispin said with a grin.

Bond cocked an eyebrow, sensing the small comma of hair had fallen over his right temple. 'If there's anything left of me to boil.'

As he said it, Bond had a strange premonition of an unsuspected impending disaster.

'VIP treatment.' Sukie sounded delighted when she saw the executive jet. 'Just like the old days with Pasquale.'

Nannie simply took it in her stride. Within minutes they were buckled into their seat belts, whining down the runway and lifting into the black hole of the night. The steward came round with drinks and sandwiches, then discreetly left them alone.

'So, for the umpteenth time, where are we going, James?' Sukie asked as she raised her glass.

'And what's more to the point, why?' said Nannie, sipping her mineral water.

'The where is Florida. Miami first, and then on south. The why's more difficult.'

'Try us,' Nannie said with a smile, peering over the top of her granny glasses.

'Oh, we've had a rotten apple in the barrel. Someone I trusted. He set me up, so now I've set him up, arranged a small diversion so that his people think we're all on the way to Paris. In fact, as you can see, we're travelling in some style to Zurich. From there we go by courtesy of Pan American Airlines to Miami. First class, of course, but I suggest we separate once we reach Zurich. So here are your tickets, ladies.'

He opened the envelope given him by Crispin and handed over the long blue and white folders containing the Zurich-Miami flight reservations made out in their real names, the Principessa Sukie Tempesta and Miss Nannette Norrich. He held back the Providence and Boston Airlines tickets that would get them from Miami to Key West. For some reason he sensed it was better not to let them know the final destination until the last minute. He also glanced at his own ticket to check it was in the name of Mr J. Boldman, the alias used on his B passport, in which he was described as a company director. Everything appeared to be in order.

They arranged to disembark separately at Zurich, to travel independently on the Pan Am flight and to meet up again by the Delta Airlines desk in the main building at Miami International.

'Get a Skycap to take you there,' Bond advised them. 'The place is vast and you can easily get lost. And beware of legal panhandlers – Hare Krishna, nuns, whatever, they're . . .'

'Thick on the ground,' finished Nannie. 'We know, James, we've been to Miami before.'

'Sorry. Right, we're set then. If either of you have second thoughts . . .'

'We've been over that as well. We're going to see it through,' said Nannie firmly.

'To the bitter end, James.' Sukie leaned forward and covered his hand with her own. Bond nodded.

He caught sight of the pair at Zurich having a snack in one of the splendid cafés that seem to litter that clean and pleasant airport. Bond drank coffee and ate a croissant before checking in for the Pan Am flight.

On the 747, Sukie and Nannie were seated right up in the front, while Bond occupied a window seat some way behind on the starboard side. Neither gave him a second look. He admired the way Sukie had so quickly picked up field technique; Nannie he almost took for granted, for she had already shown how good she could be.

The food was reasonable, the flight boring, the movie violent and cut to ribbons. It was hot and crowded when they landed at Miami International, soon after eight in the evening. Sukie and Nannie were already at the Delta desk when he reached it.

'Okay,' he greeted them. 'Now we go through Gate E to the PBA departures.'

He handed them the tickets for the final flight.

'Key West?' queried Nannie.

'The Last Resort, they call it,' said Sukie, laughing. 'Great. I've been there.'

'Well, I want to arrive . . .'

The ping-pong of an announcement signal interrupted him. He opened his mouth to continue, expecting it to be a routine call for some departure, but the voice mentioned the name Boldman.

'Would Mr James Boldman, passenger recently arrived from Zurich, report to the information desk opposite the British Airways counter. Mr Boldman, please.'

Bond shrugged. 'I was going to say that I wanted to arrive incognito. Well, that's my incognito. There must be some development from my people. Wait for me.'

He pressed his way through queues of people and baggage waiting to be checked in. At the information desk a blonde with teeth in gloss white and lips in blood red batted her eyelids at him.

'Can I help y'awl?'

'Message for James Boldman,' he said, and saw her glance behind his left shoulder and nod.

The voice was soft in his ear, and unmistakable.

'Good evening, Mr Boldman. Nice to see you.'

Steve Quinn pressed close as Bond turned. He could feel the pistol muzzle hard against his ribs, and knew his face to be etched with surprise.

'How nice for us to be meeting again, Mr – what do you call yourself now – Boldman?' Doktor Kirchtum stood on his right, his big face moulded into what appeared to be a big smile of welcome.

'What . . .' Bond began.

'Just start walking quietly out of the exit doors over there.' Quinn's smile didn't change. 'Forget your travelling companions and the PBA flight. We're going to Key West by a different route.'

14

FROST-FREE CITY

The aircraft was very quiet in flight. Only a low rumbling whine from the jets was audible. Bond, who had managed no more than a quick look before boarding, thought it was probably an Aerospatiale Corvette, with its distinctive long nose. The interior was decorated in blue and gold, with six swivel armchairs and a long central table.

Outside there was darkness, with only the occasional pin of light flashing in the distance. Bond guessed they were now high over the Everglades, or turning to make the run in to Key West across the sea.

The initial shock of finding himself flanked by Quinn and Kirchtum had passed very quickly. One learned to react instantly in his job. In this situation he had no option but to go along with Quinn's instructions: it was his only chance of survival.

There had been a moment's hesitation when he first felt the gun pressing into his ribs. Then he obeyed, walking calmly between the two big men who kept close beside him, as though making a discreet arrest. Now he was really on his own. The other two had their tickets to Key West, but he had told them to wait for him. They also had all the luggage, and his case contained the weapons – Nannie's two little automatics, the ASP, and the baton.

A long black limousine with tinted windows stood parked directly outside the exit. Kirchtum moved forward a pace to open the rear door, bent his heavy body and entered first.

'In!' Quinn prodded Bond with the gun, almost pushing him into the leather-scented interior and quickly following him so that he was sandwiched between the two men.

The motor was started before the door slammed shut, and the vehicle pulled smoothly away from the kerb. Quinn had the gun out now – a small Makarov, Russian made and based on the German Walther PP series design. Bond recognised it immediately, even in the dim glow thrown into the car from the airport lights. By the same light he could see the driver's head, like a large, elongated coconut, topped with a peaked cap. Nobody spoke, and no orders were given. The limousine purred on to a slip-road which, Bond guessed, led to the airport perimeter tracks.

'Not a word, James,' Quinn whispered, 'on your life, and on May's and Moneypenny's as well.'

They were approaching large gates set into a high chain-link fence.

The car stopped at a security shed and Bond heard the electronic whine as the driver's window was lowered. A guard approached. The driver offered him a clutch of identity cards and the guard muttered something. The nearside rear window slid down and the guard peered in, looking at the cards in his hand and then glancing in at Quinn, Bond and Kirchtum.

'Okay,' he said at last in a gravel drawl. 'Through the gate and wait for the guide truck.'

They moved forward and stopped, lights dipped. Somewhere ahead of them there was a mighty roar as an aircraft landed, its reverse thrust blanketing all other sounds. Dimmed lights appeared as a small truck performed a neat turn in front of them. It was painted with yellow stripes and a red light revolved on the canopy. The rear carried a large 'Follow me' sign.

Keeping behind the truck, the car moved slowly past aircraft of all types – commercial jets being loaded and unloaded, large piston-engined aeroplanes, freighters, small private craft, the insignias ranging from Pan Am, British Airways, and Delta to

Datsun and Island City Flying Service. They made for an aircraft that stood apart from the rest near a cluster of buildings on the far side of the field, pulling up so close that Bond thought for a moment they might touch the wing.

For large men, Quinn and Kirchtum moved fast. Like a well-drilled team, Kirchtum left the car almost before it had come to a standstill, while Quinn edged Bond towards the door, so that he was constantly covered from both sides. Once in the open, Kirchtum kept a steel grip on his arm until Quinn was out. Using an arm-lock, they forced him up the steps and into the aeroplane. Quinn's pistol was now in full view as Kirchtum hauled in the steps and closed the door with a solid thud.

'That seat.' Quinn indicated with the pistol. Kirchtum placed handcuffs on each of Bond's wrists, which he then attached to small steel D-rings in the padded arms of the seat.

'You've done this before,' Bond said, smiling. There was no edge in showing fear to people like this.

'Just a precaution. It would be foolish to be forced to use this once we're airborne.'

Quinn stood clear, the pistol levelled, as Kirchtum looped shackles around Bond's ankles, and secured them to similar steel D-rings on the lower part of the seat. The engines rumbled into life and seconds later they were moving. There was a short wait as they taxied in line, then the little jet swung on to the runway, burst into full life and roared away, climbing fast.

'I apologise for the deception, James.' Quinn was now relaxed and leaning back in his seat with a drink. 'You see, we thought you might just visit the Mozart, so we stayed prepared – even with the torture paraphernalia on show, and the Herr Doktor looking like an unwilling victim. I admit to one serious error: I should have ordered my outside team to move in after you entered. However, these things happen. The Doktor was excellent in his role of frightened captive, I thought.'

'Oscar nominee.' Bond's expression did not alter. 'I hope nothing nasty is going to happen to my two lady friends.'

'I don't think you need bother yourself about them,' said Quinn, smiling happily. 'We sent them a message that you would not be leaving tonight. They think you're joining them at the Airport Hilton. I expect they're waiting there for you now. If they do get suspicious, I'm afraid they won't be able to do much about it. You have a date around lunchtime tomorrow with what the good old French revolutionaries called Madame La Guillotine. I shall not be there to witness it. As I told you, we have orders only to hand you over to SPECTRE. We take the money and see to the release of May and Moneypenny – you can trust me over that. They will be returned unopened. Even though it would have been useful to interrogate Moneypenny.'

'And where is all this going to take place?' Bond asked, his voice betraying no concern about his appointment with the guillotine.

'Oh, quite near Key West. A few miles offshore. Outside the reef. Unfortunately our timing isn't brilliant – we'll have to hole up with you until dawn. The channel through the reef is not the easiest to navigate, and we don't want to end up on a sandbar. But we'll manage. I promised my superiors I would hand you over and I like to keep my promises.'

'Especially to the kind of masters you serve,' Bond replied. 'Failure isn't exactly appreciated in the Russian service. At best you'd be demoted, or end up running exercises for trainees; at worst it would be one of those nice hospitals where they inject you with Aminazin – such a pleasant drug. Turns you into a living vegetable. I reckon that's exactly how you'll end up.' He turned to Kirchtum. 'You too, Herr Doktor. How did they put the arm on you?'

The doctor shrugged.

'The Klinik Mozart is my whole life, Mr Bond. My entire life. Some years ago we had – how do I put it? A financial embarrassment . . .'

'You were broke,' Bond said placidly.

'So. *Ja*. Broke. No funds. Friends of Mr Quinn – the people he works for – made me a very good offer. I could carry on my work, which has always been in the interests of humanity, and they would see to the funds.'

'I can guess the rest,' Bond cut in. 'The price was your coopera-tion. The odd visitor to be kept under sedation for a while. Sometimes a body. Occasionally some surgery.'

The doctor nodded sadly. 'Yes, all those things. I admit that I did not expect to become involved in a situation like the present one. But Mr Quinn tells me I shall be able to return with no blot on my professional character. Officially I am away for two days. A rest.'

Bond laughed. 'A rest? You believe that? It can only end up with arrest, Herr Doktor. Either arrest, or one of Mr Quinn's bullets. Probably the latter.'

'Stop that,' Quinn said sharply. 'The doctor has been a great help. He will be rewarded, and he knows it.' He smiled at Kirchtum. 'Mr Bond is using an old, old trick, trying to make you doubt our intentions, attempting to drive a wedge between us. You know how clever he can be. You've seen him in action.'

Again the doctor nodded. '*Ja*. The shooting of Vasili and Yuri was not funny. That I did not like.'

'But you were also clever. You gave Mr Quinn some harmless injection . . .'

'Saline.'

'And then you must have followed me.'

'We were on your track very quickly,' Quinn said flatly as he glanced towards the window. Outside there was still darkness. 'But you changed my plans. My people in Paris were supposed to deal with you. It took some very fast and fancy choreography to arrange this, James. But we managed.'

'You did indeed.'

Bond swivelled his seat, leaning forward to see out of the window. He thought there were lights in the distance.

'Ah.' Quinn sounded pleased. 'There we are. Lights – Stock Island and Key West. About ten minutes to go, I'd say.'

'And what if I make a fuss when we land?'

'You won't make a fuss.'

'You're very confident.'

'I have an insurance. Just as you had with me, because of Tabitha. I really do believe you will do as you're told to secure the release of May and Moneypenny. It's the one chink in your armour, James. Always has been. Yes, you're a cold fish; ruthless. But you're also an old-fashioned English gentleman at heart. You'd give your life to save a defenceless woman and this time we're talking of two women – your own ageing housekeeper and your Chief's Personal Assistant, who has been hopelessly devoted to you for years. People you care for most in the world. Of course you'll give your life for them. Unhappily, it's in your nature. Unhappily, did I say? I really meant happily – for us, happily.'

Bond swallowed. Deep down inside he knew that Steve Quinn had played the trump card. He was right. 007 would go to his own death to save the lives of people like May and Moneypenny.

'There's another reason why you won't make a fuss.' It was hard to detect Quinn's smile under that bushy beard, and it did not show in his eyes. 'Show him, Herr Doktor.'

Kirchtum lifted a small case which lay in the magazine rack between the seats. From it he drew out what looked like a child's space gun made of clear plastic.

'This is an injection pistol,' Kirchtum explained. 'Before we land I shall fill it. Look, you can see the action.'

He drew back a small plunger from the rear, lifted the barrel in front of Bond's face and touched the tiny trigger. The instrument was no more than seven centimetres long, with about five for the butt. As he touched the trigger, a hypodermic needle appeared from the muzzle.

'An injection is given in 2.5 seconds.' The doctor nodded

gravely. 'Very quick. Also the needle is very long. Goes easily through cloth.'

'You show the least sign of making a fuss, and you get the needle, right?'

'Instant death.'

'Oh, no. Instant facsimile heart attack. You'll come back to us within half an hour, as good as new. SPECTRE want your head. In the final resort, we would kill you with a power tool. But we'd rather deliver your whole body alive and intact. We owe Rahani a few favours, and the poor man hasn't long to live. Your head is his last request.'

A moment later the pilot came on the intercom system to ask for seatbelts to be fastened and cigarettes extinguished. He announced that they would be landing in about four minutes. Bond watched out of the window as they dropped towards the lights. He saw water and tropical vegetation interspersed with roads and low buildings coming up to meet them.

'Interesting place, Key West,' mused Quinn. 'Hemingway once called it the poor man's St Tropez. Tennessee Williams lived here too. President Truman established a little White House near what used to be the Naval Base and John F. Kennedy brought the British PM, Harold Macmillan, to visit it. Cuban boat people landed here, but long before that it was a pirates' and wreckers' paradise. I'm told it's still a smugglers' heaven, and the US Coastguard operates a tight schedule out of here.'

They swept in over the threshold and touched down with hardly a bump.

'There's history in this airport as well,' Quinn continued. 'First regular US mail flight started from here; and Key West is both the beginning and end of Highway Route One.' They rolled to a halt, then began to taxi towards a shack-like hut with a veranda. Bond saw a low wall with faded lettering: 'Welcome to Key West the Only Frost-Free City in the United States'.

'And they have the most spectacular sunsets,' Quinn added. 'Really incredible. Pity you won't be around to see one.'

The heat hit them like a furnace as they left the aircraft. Even the mild breeze felt as if it was blowing from an inferno.

The departure from the jet was as carefully organised as the boarding, with Kirchtum close enough to use his deadly little syringe at any moment, should Bond alert their suspicion.

'Smile and pretend to talk,' muttered Quinn, glancing towards the veranda where a dozen or so people were waiting to welcome passengers off a newly arrived PBA flight. Bond scanned the faces, but recognised nobody. They passed through a small gate in the wall beside the shack, Quinn and Kirchtum pushing him towards another sleek dark automobile. In a few moments, Bond was again seated between the two men. This time the driver was young, in an open-necked shirt and with long blond hair.

'Y'awl okay?'

'Just drive,' Quinn snapped. 'There's a place arranged I understand.'

'Sure thing. Git y'there in no time.' He drew out on to the road, turning his head slightly. 'Y'awl mind if'n I have some music playin'?'

'Go ahead. As long as it doesn't frighten the horses.'

Quinn was very relaxed and confident. If it had not been for Kirchtum, tense on the other side, Bond would have made a move. But the doctor was wound up like a hair trigger. He would have the hypo into 007 if he moved a muscle. A burst of sound filled the car, a rough voice singing, tired, cynical and sad:

> There's a hole in Daddy's arm,
> Where all the money goes . . .

'Not that!' cracked Quinn.

'Ah'm sorry. I kinda like rock and roll. Rhythm and blues. Man, it's good music.'

'I said not that.'

The car went silent, the driver sullen. Bond watched the signs – South Roosevelt Boulevard, a restaurant alive with people eating, Martha's. There were wooden, clapboard houses, white with fretted gingerbread decorations along the porches and verandas; lights flashing – Motel; No vacancy. Lush tropical foliage lined the road, with the ocean on their right. They appeared to be following a long bend taking them away from the Atlantic. Then they turned suddenly at a sign to Searstown. Bond saw they were in a large shopping area.

The car pulled up beside a supermarket alive with late shoppers and an optometrist's. Between the two lay a narrow alley.

'It's up there. Door on the right. Up above the eye place, where they sell reading glasses. Guess y'awl want me to pick you up.'

'Five o'clock,' Quinn said quietly. 'In time to get to Garrison Bight at dawn.'

'Y'awl goin' on a fishin' trip, then?'

The driver turned round and Bond saw his face for the first time. He was not a young man, as Bond had thought, despite the long blond hair. Half his face was missing, sunken in and patched with skin grafts. He must have sensed Bond's shock for he looked at him straight with his one good eye, and gave an ugly grimace.

'Don't you worry about me none. That's why I work for these gentlemen here. I got this brand new face in Nam, so I thought I could put it to use. Frightens the hell outa some folks.'

'Five o'clock,' Quinn repeated, opening the door.

The routine did not vary. They had Bond out, along the alley, through a door and up one flight of stairs in a few seconds. They had brought him to a bare room. In it were only two chairs and two beds, flimsy curtains and a noisy air-conditioning unit. Again they used the handcuffs and shackles, and Kirchtum sat close to Bond, the hypodermic in his hand, while Quinn went out for food. They ate melon and some bread and ham, washing it down with mineral water. Then Quinn and Kirchtum took turns in guarding Bond, who, resigned, fell asleep with exhaustion.

It was still dark when Quinn shook him awake. He stood over Bond in the bare, functional little bathroom as he tried to fight off the grogginess of travel. After about ten minutes they led him downstairs to the car.

There were few signs of life so early in the morning. The sky looked hard and grey, but Quinn said it was going to be a beautiful day. They came to North Roosevelt Boulevard, then passed a marina on their left with yachts and big powered fishing boats moored. Water appeared on the right as well. Quinn pointed.

'That's where we'll be heading. The Gulf of Mexico. The island's out on the far side of the reef.'

At the Harbour Lights restaurant sign Bond was hustled out of the car, along the side of the sleeping restaurant and down on to the marina quayside. A tall, muscular man waited beside a large, powered fishing boat with a high laddered and skeletal superstructure above the cabin. The engines were idling.

Quinn and the captain exchanged nods, and they pushed Bond aboard and down into the narrow cabin. Once more the handcuffs and shackles were put on. The noise of the engine rose, and Bond could feel the swell as the craft started out from the quayside, cruising into the marina and under a bridge. As the boat picked up speed, Kirchtum grew calmer. He put away the hypodermic. Quinn joined the captain at the controls.

Five minutes out, they had really started to make way, the boat rolling slightly and bounding, slapping hard down into the water. Everyone appeared to be concentrating on the navigation, and Bond began to think seriously about his predicament. They had spoken of an island outside the reef, and he wondered how long it would take them to reach it. He then concentrated on the handcuffs realising that there was little he could do to get out of them. Unexpectedly, Quinn came down into the cabin.

'I'm going to gag you and cover you up.' Then he spoke to Kirchtum and Bond just made out what he was saying. 'There's another fishing boat to starboard . . . appears to be in some kind of trouble . . . The captain says we should offer to help . . . they could report us. I don't want to raise suspicion.'

He pushed a handkerchief into Bond's mouth and tied another around it, so that, for a moment he thought he would suffocate. Then, after checking the shackles, Quinn threw a blanket over him. In the darkness, Bond listened. They were slowing, rolling a little, but definitely slowing.

Above, he heard the captain shouting, 'You in trouble?' Then, a few seconds later, 'Right, I'll come aboard, but I have an RV. May have to pick you up on the way back.'

There was a sharp bump, as though they had made contact with the other boat, and then all hell broke loose. Bond lost count after the first dozen shots. There were the cracks of hand guns followed by the stutter of a machine pistol; then a cry, which sounded like Kirchtum, and thumps on the deck above. Then silence, until he heard the sound of bare feet descending into the cabin.

The blanket was hauled back roughly and Bond tried to turn his head, eyes widening as he saw the figure above him. Nannie Norrich had her small automatic in one hand.

'Well, well, Master James, we do have to get you out of some scrapes, don't we?' She turned her head. 'Sukie, it's okay. He's down here, trussed up and oven-ready by the look of it.'

Sukie appeared, also armed. She grinned appealingly.

'Bondage, they call it, I believe.'

She began to laugh as Bond let off a stream of obscenities which were completely incomprehensible from behind the gag. Nannie wrenched at the handcuffs and shackles. Sukie went aloft again, returning with keys.

'I hope those idiots weren't friends of yours,' said Nannie. 'I'm afraid we had to deal with them.'

'What do you mean, "deal"?' Bond spluttered as the gag came away. She looked so innocent that his blood ran cold.

'I'm afraid they're dead, James. All three of them. Stone dead. But you must admit, we were clever to find *you*.'

15

THE PRICE FOR A LIFE

Bond felt an odd sense of shock that two relatively young women had brought about the carnage he saw on the deck, yet could remain buoyant, even elated, as though killing three men was like swatting flies in a kitchen. He also realised that he was suffering from a certain amount of resentment – he had taken the initiative, he had been duped by Quinn and Kirchtum, he had fallen into their quickly devised trap. Yet he had not been able to effect his own escape. These mere women had rescued him, and he felt resentful – a peculiar reaction when he should have been grateful.

Another, almost identical powered fishing boat bearing the name *Prospero* lay alongside, rising, falling and gently bumping against their vessel. They were well outside the reef. In the far distance little low mounds of islands rose from the sea. The sky was turning from pearl to deep blue as the sun cleared the horizon. Quinn had been right. It was going to be a beautiful day.

'Well?'

Nannie stood near him, looking around while Sukie appeared to be busying herself on the other boat.

'Well what?' Bond asked flatly.

'Well, weren't we clever to find you?'

'Very.' He sounded sharp, almost angry. 'Was all this necessary?'

'You mean blowing away your captors?' The expression sounded strange coming from Nannie Norrich. She flushed with anger now. 'Yes, very necessary. Can't you even say thank you, James? We tried to deal with it peacefully, but they opened up with that damned Uzi. They gave us no option.'

She pointed towards their boat and the nasty jagged row of holes in the hull, abaft the high skeleton superstructure above the cabin.

Bond nodded, muttering his thanks.

'You were, indeed, very clever to find me. I'd like to hear more about that.'

'And so you shall,' Nannie said waspishly, 'but first we really have to do something about this mess.'

'What weapons are you carrying?'

'The two pistols from your case – your stuff's back at the hotel in Key West. I had to force the locks, I'm afraid. I couldn't work out the combinations, and we were fairly desperate by then.'

'Any extra fuel around?'

She pointed past Kirchtum's slumped corpse in the stern well. 'A couple of cans there. We've got three aboard our boat.'

'It's got to look like a catastrophe,' Bond said with a frown. 'What's more, they mustn't find the bodies. An explosion would be best – preferably when we're well out of the area. It's easy enough to do, but we must have some kind of fuse, and that's what we haven't got.'

'But we do have a signal pistol. We could use the flares.'

Bond nodded. 'Good. What's the range – about a hundred metres? You go back with Sukie and get the pistol and flares ready. I'll do what's necessary here.'

Nannie turned away, sprang lightly on to the guard rail, and jumped aboard their boat, calling cheerfully to Sukie.

Bond then set about his grim task, still preoccupied with the recent turn of events. How did they manage to find him? How could they have been in the right place at the right time? Until he had answers that satisfied him, he could not trust either of the young women.

He searched the boat carefully, assembling everything that

might be useful on the deck – rope, wire and the strong lines used for bringing in sharks and swordfish. All the weapons he threw overboard, except for Quinn's automatic, a prosaic Browning 9mm, and some spare clips.

Then came the grisly job of moving the bodies into the stern well. Kirchtum, already there, only needed turning over, which Bond managed to do with his feet; the captain's body stuck in the wheelhouse door, and he had to tug hard to get it free. Quinn was the most difficult to move, for the bloody decapitated remains had to be dragged along the narrow gap separating cabin from guard rail.

He placed the corpses in a row directly over the fuel tanks and lashed them loosely together with fishing line. He then went forward again and gathered as much inflammable material as he could find – sheets and blankets off the four cabin bunks, cushions, pillows and even pieces of rag. These he piled up well forward, weighting them with life jackets and heavier equipment. One piece of coiled rope he left near the bodies.

He transferred himself to the other boat, where he found Sukie standing in the wheelhouse with Nannie close behind her on the steps leading down to the cabin. Nannie was holding the bulbous flare projector by the muzzle.

'There it is. One flare pistol.'

'Plenty of flares?'

She pointed to a metal box containing a dozen stumpy cartridges, each marked with its colour: red, green or illuminating. Bond picked out three of the illuminating flares.

'These should do us.'

He rapidly gave them instructions, and Sukie started the engines while Nannie cast off all but one rope amidships.

Bond returned to the other boat to make the final preparations. He dragged the rope near the bodies to the pile of material, secured it underneath and gently played it out back to the stern wall, laying it alongside the inlets to the fuel tanks. He went forward again with one of the emergency fuel cans and saturated first the material, then, shuffling backwards towards the corpses, he ran plenty of the liquid over the rope.

He opened the second can to dowse the human remains in fuel, unscrewed the main fuel cap and lowered the saturated rope into the tank.

'Stand by!' he yelled.

He ran from the stern well, mounted the guard rail and was aboard the other boat just as Nannie let go of the rope amidships. Sukie slowly eased open the throttle and they pulled away, gently turning stern-on to the other boat.

Bond positioned himself aft of the superstructure, slid a flare into the pistol, checked the wind and watched the gap slowly widen between the two craft. At around eighty metres he raised the pistol high and fired an illuminating flare in a low, flat trajectory. The flare hissed right across the bows of the other boat. Bond had already reloaded and taken up another position. This time, the fizzing white flare performed a perfect arc, leaving a thick stream of white smoke behind it, to land in the bows. There was a second's pause before the material ignited with a small *whumph*. The flames were carried straight along the rope fuse towards the fuel tanks, and the bodies.

'Give her full power and weave as much as possible!' Bond shouted to Sukie.

The engine note rose, bows lifting, almost before he had finished giving the order. Rapidly they bounced away from the blazing fishing boat.

The corpses caught alight first, the stern well sending up a crimson flame and then a dense cloud of black smoke. They were a good two kilometres away when the fuel tanks went up – a great roaring explosion with a dark red centre, ripping the boat apart in a ferocious fireball. For a few moments there was the smoke and a rising cascade of debris, then nothing. The water appeared to boil around what little remained of the powerful fishing launch, then it settled, steamed for a few seconds, and flattened. The shock waves hit the rear of their boat a second or two after the explosion. There was a slight burn on the wind, which they felt on their cheeks.

At five kilometres there was nothing to be seen, but Bond remained leaning against the superstructure, gazing in the direction of the small, violent inferno.

'Coffee?' Nannie asked.

'Depends how long we're staying at sea.'

'We hired this boat for a day's fishing,' she said. 'I don't think we should raise suspicion.'

'No, we'll even have to try and fish. Is Sukie okay at the wheel?'

Sukie Tempesta turned and nodded, smiling.

'She's sailed boats all her life.' Nannie gestured towards the steps leading below. 'There's coffee on . . .'

'And I want to hear how you managed to find me,' Bond said, staring at her steadily.

'I told you. I was minding you, James.'

They were now seated on the bunks in the cramped cabin, facing each other. They nursed mugs of coffee as the boat rolled and the sea thudded against the hull. Sukie had reduced power and they seemed to be performing a series of gentle, wide circles.

'When Norrich Universal Bodyguards take it upon themselves to look after you, you get looked after.'

Nannie had her long legs tucked under her on the bunk, and had unpinned her hair so that it fell, dark and thick, to her shoulders, giving her face an almost elfin look, and somehow making the grey eyes softer and very interesting. Take care, Bond thought, this lady has to explain herself, and she had better be convincing.

'So I got looked after.' He did not smile.

She explained that as soon as he had been paged at Miami International she had left Sukie with the luggage and followed him at a discreet distance.

'I had plenty of cover – you know how crowded the place was – but I saw the routine. I'm experienced enough to know when a client is being pulled.'

'But they took me away by car.'

'Yes. I got its number and then made a quick call – my little NUB has a small branch here, and they put a trace on the limo. I said I'd call them back if I needed assistance. After that I called the flight planning office.'

'Resourceful lady.'

'James, in this game you have to be. Apart from the scheduled flights to Key West there was one private exec jet that had filed a flight plan. I took down the details . . .'

'Which were?'

'Company called Société pour la Promotion de l'Écologie et de la Civilisation . . .'

SPEC, Bond thought, SPEC. SPECTRE.

'We had about six minutes to catch the PBA flight to Key West, so I gambled that we'd make it just before the private flight.'

'You also gambled on my being on board the SPEC jet.'

She nodded. 'Yes, and you were. If you hadn't been, I would have had egg on my face. As it happened, we were off the aircraft a good five minutes before you came along. I even had time to hire a car, send Sukie to book into the hotel and follow you to that shopping centre in Searstown.'

'And then what?'

'I hung around.' She paused, not looking at him. 'To be honest, I didn't really know what to do. Then, like a small miracle, the big bearded guy came out and went straight to the telephone booth. I was only a few paces away and I've got good eyesight. Don't be fooled by the spectacles. I watched him punch out a number and talk for a while. When he went to the supermarket I slipped into the booth and dialled the number. He had called the Harbour Lights restaurant.'

There was a street guide in the little rented Volkswagen, and the Harbour Lights was easy enough to find. 'As soon as I got inside I realised it was a fishing and sailing place, full of bronzed, muscular men renting boats, and themselves to sail them. I just asked around. One man – the one who went up in smoke just now – mentioned that he had been hired for an early start. He'd had a bit to drink and even told me what time he was leaving, and that he had three passengers.'

'So you hired another powered fishing launch.'

'That's right. I told the captain I didn't need help. Sukie can navigate the trickiest waters blindfold and with her hands tied. He took me down to this boat, made a pass and got the push. But he did show me the charts, and told me about the currents and channels, which are not easy. He talked about the reef, the islands and the drop-off into the Gulf of Mexico.'

'So you went back to Sukie at the hotel . . .'

'And pored over the charts half the night. We got down to Garrison Bight early and were outside the reef when your boat came out. We watched you on the radar. Then we positioned ourselves near enough to your course, stopped the engines and started firing distress flares. You know the rest.'

'You tried the soft approach, but they opened up with the Uzi.'

'To their cost.' She cocked her head, and gave a sigh. 'Lord, I'm tired.'

'You're not alone. And what about Sukie?'

'She seems happy enough. She always is with boats.' Nannie put down her empty coffee mug and started slowly to undo the buttons of her shirt. 'I really think I'd like to lie down, James. Would you like to lie down with me?'

'What if we hit a squall? We'll be thrown all over the place.' Bond leaned forward to kiss her gently on the mouth.

'I'd rather meet a swell.' Her arms came up around his neck, drawing him towards her.

Later, she said that she'd rarely been thanked so well for saving somebody's life.

'You should do it again sometime.'

Bond kissed her, running one hand over her naked body.

'Why not now?' asked Nannie with an implike grin. 'It seems a fair price for a life.'

16

GOING DOWN TONIGHT

'As far as I can tell, there are three islands outside the reef that are privately owned and have some kind of building on them.' Sukie's finger roamed around the chart of the Key West vicinity.

It was early afternoon, and they were hove to with fishing lines out. Four large red snapper had come their way, but nothing big – no sharks or swordfish.

'This one here,' said Sukie, indicating an island just outside the reef, 'is owned by the man who built the hotel where we're staying. There's another to the north, and this one,' her finger circled a large patch of land, 'just on the shelf, before you reach the drop-off. The continental shelf suddenly drops down from 270 metres to over 600. Great fishing water around the drop-off. There have been treasure seekers by the dozen in the area too.' She prodded the island on the map. 'Anyway, it looked very much as though that was where you were heading.'

Bond peered closer to see the name. 'Shark Island,' he said. 'How cosy.'

'Someone seems to think so. I asked around the hotel last night. A couple of years ago a man who called himself Rainey, Tarquin Rainey, bought the place. The boy at the hotel is from an old Key West family and knows all the gossip. He says this fellow Rainey is a mystery man. He arrives by private jet and gets ferried out to Shark Island by helicopter, or by a launch which belongs to the place. He's also a bit of a go-getter. People who build on the islands usually take a lot of time; it's always difficult getting the materials taken out to them. Rainey had his place up in the space of one summer and the island landscaped in the second summer. He's got tropical trees, gardens, the lot. They're very impressed, the people in Key West, and it takes a great deal to impress them, particularly as they claim to be a republic. The Conch Republic.'

She pronounced it 'Konk'.

'Nobody's seen him?' Bond asked, knowing that the alias Tarquin Rainey could not be a coincidence. The man had to be Tamil Rahani, which meant Shark Island was SPECTRE property.

'I believe a few people have had glimpses of him – at a distance. Nobody's encouraged to get near him, though. Apparently some people have approached Shark Island by boat and been warned away, politely, but very firmly, by large men in fast motor boats.'

'Mmmmm.' Bond thought for a few moments, then asked Sukie if she could navigate to within a couple of kilometres at night.

'If the charts are accurate, yes. It'll be slow going, but it's possible. When did you want to go?'

'I thought perhaps tonight. If that's where I was being taken, it's only common courtesy for me to call on Mr Rainey at the earliest possible opportunity.'

Bond gazed steadily first at Sukie and then at Nannie, both of whom looked very dubious about the idea.

'I think we should head back to Garrison Bight now,' he went on. 'See if you can keep the boat for a couple of days longer. I'll get myself a few bits and pieces I'm going to need. We could have a look around Key West – see and be seen. We'll set out for Shark Island at about two in the morning. I won't put you in danger, that I promise. You simply wait offshore and if I don't return by a certain time, you get the hell out and come back tomorrow night.'

'Okay by me,' said Sukie as she got to her feet.

Nannie just nodded. She had been quiet since they had come

back on deck. Occasionally she would shoot warm glances in Bond's direction.

'Right. Let's get the lines hauled in,' he said decisively. 'We sail at two. In the meantime, there's a great deal to be done.'

The local police were at Garrison Bight when they returned, checking on the boat hired by Steve Quinn. There had been a report from another power boat which had seen a plume of smoke, and from a naval helicopter that had spotted wreckage. They had seen it themselves an hour or so after Quinn's boat had exploded and had even waved to it, knowing they were well away from Quinn's vessel.

Nannie went ashore and talked to the police, while Sukie stayed in sight on deck and Bond remained in the cabin. After half an hour Nannie returned, saying she had charmed the pants off the cops and had hired the boat for a week.

'I hope we're not going to need it that long,' Bond said with a grimace.

'Better safe than sorry, as we nannies say.' She poked her tongue out before adding, 'Master James.'

'I've had enough of that little joke, thank you.' He sounded genuinely irritated. 'Now, where are we staying?'

'There's only one place to stay in Key West,' Sukie put in. 'The Pier House Hotel. You get a wonderful view of the famous sunset from there.'

'I've a lot to do before sunset,' Bond said sharply. 'The sooner we get to this – what's it called? Pier House – the better.'

As they set off in the hired Volkswagen, Bond suddenly felt very naked without a weapon of any kind. He sat next to Nannie, with Sukie, who had been here before, squeezed into the back giving an occasional commentary.

To Bond, the place was an odd mixture of tourist resort garishness and pockets of great beauty, with areas of luxury which spelled money. It was hot, palm trees shimmered and moved in the light breeze, and they passed numerous clapboard gingerbread houses, which were bright and well painted, their yards and gardens filled with the colour of subtropical flowers. Yet well-kept houses could be adjacent to rubbish tips. The sidewalks were in fine order in one street, in the next cracked, broken or almost non-existent.

At an intersection, they had to wait for an extraordinary-looking train – a kind of model railroad engine built on to a diesel-powered jeep, which pulled a series of cars full of people under striped awnings.

'The Conch Train,' Sukie informed them. 'That's the way tourists get to see Key West.'

Bond could hear the driver, all done out in blue overalls and peaked cap, going through a litany of the sights and their history as the train wound its way around the island.

They finally turned into a long street of wood and concrete buildings, which appeared to house nothing but jewellery, tourist junk and art shops, interspersed with prosperous-looking restaurants.

'Duval,' announced Sukie. 'It goes right down to the ocean – to our hotel in fact. It's great at night. There, that's the famous Fast Buck Freddie's Department Store. And there's Antonia's, a great Italian restaurant. Sloppy Joe's Bar was Ernest Hemingway's favourite haunt when he lived here.'

Even if Bond had not read *To Have and Have Not* he could not now have escaped knowing that Hemingway had lived in Key West. There were souvenir T-shirts and drawings of him everywhere, and Sloppy Joe's Bar proclaimed it loudly, not just from an inn sign but also on a tall painted legend on the wall.

As they reached the bottom of Duval, Bond saw what he was looking for and noted that it was a very short walk from the hotel.

'You're already registered, and your luggage is in your suite,' Nannie told him, as she parked the car. They hustled him through the light main reception area furnished in bamboo and through an enclosed courtyard where a fountain played on flowers and the tall wooden statue of a naked woman. Above, large fans revolved silently, sending a down draught of cool air.

He followed them down a passage and out into the gardens, along twisting flower-bordered pathways, with a pool deck to the left. Beyond, a line of wood and bamboo bars and restaurants ran beside a small beach. The pier the hotel was named after stretched out over the water on big wooden piles.

The building appeared to be U-shaped, with the gardens and pool in the centre of the U. They entered the main hotel again at the far side of the pool and took the elevator up one floor to two adjacent suites.

'We're sharing,' said Sukie, inserting her key into one of the doors. 'But you're right next to us, James, in case there's anything we can do for you.'

For the first time since they had met, Bond thought he could detect an invitation in Sukie's voice. He certainly saw a small angry flash in Nannie's eyes. Could it be that they were fighting over him?

'What's the plan?' Nannie asked, a little sharply.

'Where's the best place to watch this incredible sunset?'

She allowed him a smile. 'The deck outside the Havana Docks bar, or so they tell me.'

'And at what time?'

'Around six.'

'The bar's in the hotel?'

'Right over there.' She waved a hand vaguely in the direction from which they had come. 'Above the restaurants, right out towards the sea.'

'Meet you both there at six, then.'

Bond smiled, turned the key in his door and disappeared into a pleasant and functional, if not luxurious, suite.

The two briefcases stood with his special Samsonite folding case in the middle of the room. It took Bond less than ten minutes to complete his unpacking. He felt better with the ASP hidden away under his jacket, and the baton at his waistband.

He checked the rooms carefully, made certain the window catches were secure, then quietly opened the door. The corridor was deserted. Silently he closed the door, making his way quickly to the elevator and back down into the gardens, using an exit to the car park which he had noticed on the way through. It was hot and humid outside.

At the far end of the parking lot stood a low building called the Pier House Market, with access from both the hotel and Front Street. Bond went straight through, pausing for a moment to look at the fruit and meat on sale, then on Front Street he turned right and crossed the cracked and lumpy road, walking fast to the corner of Duval. He passed the shop he really wanted to visit and bought some faded jeans, a T-shirt free of tasteless slogans and a pair of soft loafers in a male boutique. He also selected an over-priced short linen jacket. For anyone in Bond's job, a jacket or blouse was always necessary to hide the hardware.

He came out of the boutique and made his way back to the place he had spotted from the car. It had a walk-in front with a dummy clad in Scuba gear out on the sidewalk. The sign read 'Reef Plunderers' Diving Emporium'. A bearded salesman tried to sell him a three and a half hour snorkelling trip on a dive boat predictably called *Reef Plunderer II*, but Bond said he was not interested.

'Captain Jack knows all the best places to dive along the reef,' the salesman protested limply.

'I want a wet suit, snorkelling mask, knife, flippers and under-sea torch. And I shall need a shoulder bag for the lot,' Bond told him in that effectively quiet but firm tone.

The salesman looked at Bond, took in the physique under the lightweight suit and the hard look in the icy blue eyes.

'Yes, siree. Sure. Right,' he said, leading the way to the rear of the shop. 'Gonna cost a ransom, but you sure know what y'awl're after.'

'That's right.' Bond did not allow his voice to rise above the almost whispering softness.

'Right,' the salesman repeated. He was dressed to look like an old salt, with a striped T-shirt and jeans. A gold ring hung piratically rather than fashionably from one ear. He gave Bond another sidelong look and began to collect the equipment from the back of the store. It was more than a quarter of an hour before Bond was completely satisfied. He added a belt with a waterproof zipper bag to his purchases, and then paid with his Platinum Amex Card, made out in the name of James Boldman.

'Guess I'll have to just run a check on this, sir, Mr Boldman.'

'You don't have to, and you know it.' Bond gazed at the man with ice-cold eyes. 'But if you're about to make telephone calls, I'm going to stand next to you. Right?'

'Right. Right,' the pirate salesman repeated, leading the way to a tiny office at the back of the store. 'Yes, sir-bub. Yes, siree.' He picked up the telephone and dialled the Amex number. The card was cleared in seconds. It took another ten minutes for the purchases to be stowed away in the shoulder bag. As he left, Bond put his mouth very close to the pierced ear with the ring in it.

'Tell you what,' he began. 'I'm a stranger in town, but now you know my name.'

'Sure.' The pirate gave him a trapped look.

'If anyone else gets to know I've been here except you, Amex and myself, I shall come back, cut that ring from your ear and then do the same job on your nose, followed by a more vital organ.' He dropped his hand, fist clenched, so that it lay level with the pirate's crotch. 'You understand me? I mean it.'

'I already forgot your name, Mr . . . er . . . Mr . . .'

'Keep it like that,' said Bond as he strode off.

He made his way back to the hotel at the more leisurely pace of the people thronging the street. Back in his suite, he lugged the CC500 from its briefcase, hooked it to the telephone and put in a quick call to London. He did not wait for a response, but gave them his exact location, saying he would be in touch as soon as the job was completed.

'It's going down tonight,' he finished. 'If I'm not in touch within forty-eight hours, look for Shark Island, off Key West. Repeat, it's going down tonight.'

It was a very apt phrase, he thought, as he changed into his newly acquired clothes. The ASP and baton were in place, so he no longer felt naked, but, surveying himself in the mirror, he thought he would blend in nicely with the tourist scene.

'Going down tonight,' he said softly to himself. Then he left for the Havana Docks bar.

17

SHARK ISLAND

The deck in front of the Havana Docks bar at the Pier House is made of wooden planks, raised on several levels and has metal chairs and tables arranged to give visitors the impression that they are on board a ship at anchor. Globe lights on poles stand at intervals along the heavy wooden guard rail. It is perhaps the best vantage point in Key West, from which to watch the sun setting over the sea.

The deck was crowded and there was a buzz of light-hearted chatter. The lights had come on, attracting swarms of insects around the globes. Someone was playing *Mood Indigo* on the piano. The rails were lined with tourists eager to capture the sunset with their cameras.

As the clear sky turned to a deeper navy blue, so an occasional speedboat crossed in front of the hotel, while a light aircraft buzzed a wide circuit, its lights flashing. To the left, along the wide Mallory Square which fronts on to the ocean, jugglers, conjurers, fire eaters and acrobats performed amid a crush of people. It was the same on every fine night, a celebration of the day's end and a look towards the pleasures the night might bring.

James Bond sat at a table and gazed out to sea past the two dark green humps of Tank and Wisteria Islands. If he had any sense he would be on a boat or aeroplane moving out, he thought. He was fully aware of the danger close at hand. There could be no doubt that Tarquin Rainey was Tamil Rahani,

Blofeld's successor and that this could well be his last chance to smash SPECTRE once and for all.

'Isn't this absolutely super,' said Sukie delightedly. 'There really is nothing like it in the whole world.'

It was not clear whether she was talking about the huge shrimps they were eating with that very special tangy, hot red sauce, their Calypso Daiquiris, or the beautiful view.

The sun appeared to grow larger as it dropped slowly behind Wisteria Island, throwing a huge patch of blood-red light across the sky.

Above them, a US Customs helicopter clattered its way, running from south to north, red and green lights twinkling on and off as it turned, heading towards the naval air station. Bond wondered if SPECTRE had become involved in the huge drug traffic which was reported to pass into America by this route – landing on isolated sections of the Florida Keys, to be taken inland and distributed. The Navy and Customs kept a very close eye on places like Key West.

A cheer went up, echoed from the crowd further up the coastline on Mallory Square, as the sun finally plunged into the sea, filling the whole sky with deep scarlet for a couple of minutes before the velvet darkness took over.

'What's the deal, James?' Nannie asked in almost a whisper.

They drew together, their heads lowered over the seafood. He told them that until midnight, at least, they should all be seen around.

'We'll stroll out into town, have dinner somewhere, and then come back to the hotel. Afterwards I want us each to leave separately. Don't use the car, and keep an eye out for anyone following you. Nannie, you're trained in this kind of thing so you can brief Sukie, tell her the best way to avoid suspicion. I have my own plans. The most important thing is that we rendezvous at Garrison Bight, aboard *Prospero*, around one in the morning. Okay?'

Bond noticed a small furrow of concern between Nannie's eyes. 'What then?' she asked.

'Has Sukie looked at the charts?'

'Yes and it's not the easiest trip by night.' Sukie's eyes were expressionless. 'It's a challenge, though. The sandbars are not well marked and we'll have to show a certain amount of light to begin with. Once we're beyond the reef it's not too bad.'

'Just get me to within a couple of kilometres of the island,' Bond said with a hint of authority, looking straight into her eyes.

They finished their drinks and rose to leave, sauntering casually from the deck. At the door to the bar, Bond paused and asked the others to wait for a moment. He went back to the rails and looked down into the sea. Earlier he had noticed the hotel's little pull-start speed boat making trips close to the beach. It was still there, tied up between the wooden piles of the pier. Smiling to himself, he rejoined Sukie and Nannie, and they went through the bar, where the pianist was now playing *Bewitched*. A small dance floor had been set up on the beach, and a three-man combo had started to pound out rhythms. The paths were lit by shaded lamps, and people were still swimming, diving into the floodlit pool, laughing with pleasure.

They strolled, arms linked – one on each side of Bond – down Duval, looking at shop windows and peering into the restaurants, all apparently full to capacity. A crowd stood in front of the light grey, English-looking church, staring across the road at half a dozen youngsters who were breakdancing to the music of a ghetto-blaster in front of Fast Buck Freddie's Department Store.

Eventually, they retraced their footsteps and found themselves in front of Claire, a restaurant that looked both busy and exceptionally good. They walked up to the maître d', who was hovering by a tall desk in the small garden outside the main restaurant.

'Boldman,' said Bond. 'Party of three. Eight o'clock.'

The maître d' consulted his book, looked troubled and asked when the booking had been made.

'Yesterday evening,' Bond said with conviction.

'There seems to be some error, Mr Boldman . . .' the bemused man retorted, a little too firmly for Bond's liking.

'I reserved the table specially. It's the only night we can make this week. I spoke to a young man last night and he assured me I had the table.'

'Just one moment, sir.' The maître d' disappeared into the restaurant and they could see him in agitated conversation with one of the waiters. Finally he came out, smiling. 'You're lucky, sir. We've had an unexpected cancellation . . .'

'Not lucky,' Bond said with his jaw clenched. 'We had a table reserved. You're simply giving us our table.'

'Of course, sir.'

They were shown to a corner table in a pleasant white room. Bond took a seat with his back to the wall and a good view of the entrance. The tablecloths were paper, and there were packets of crayons beside each plate. Bond doodled, drawing a skull and crossbones. Nannie had sketched something vaguely obscene, in red. She leaned forward.

'I haven't spotted anyone. Are we being watched?'

'Oh yes,' Bond said with a knowing smile as he opened the large menu. 'Two of them, working each side of the street. Possibly three. Did you notice the man in a yellow shirt and jeans, tall, black and with a lot of rings on his fingers? The other's a little chap, dark trousers, white shirt, with a tattoo on his left arm – mermaid being indecent with a swordfish, by the look of it. He's across the street now.'

'Got 'em,' Nannie said as she turned to her menu.

'Where's the third?' asked Sukie.

'An old blue Buick. Big fellow at the wheel, alone and cruising. Not easy to tell, but he's been up and down the street a lot. So have others, but he was the only one who didn't seem to take any interest in people on the sidewalks. I'd say he was the backup. Watch out for them.'

A waiter appeared and took their order. They all chose Conch chowder, the Thai beef salad and, inevitably, Key lime pie. They drank a Californian champagne, which slightly offended Bond's palate. They talked constantly, keeping off their plans for the night.

When they were out on the street again, Bond told them to be wary.

'I want you both there, on board and with nobody on your backs, by one o'clock.'

As they walked west towards the Front Street intersection, the man in the yellow shirt kept well back on the other side of the street. The tattooed man let them pass him, then overtook them and let them pass again before they got back to the Pier House. The blue Buick had cruised by twice, and was parked outside the Lobster House, almost opposite the main entrance to the hotel.

'They have us well staked out,' Bond murmured as they crossed the street and walked up the drive to the main entrance. There they made a great show of saying goodnight.

Bond was taking no chances. As soon as he got to his room he checked the old, well-tried traps he had laid. The slivers of matchstick were still wedged into the doors of the clothes cupboards and the threads on the drawers were unbroken. His luggage was also intact. It was ten-thirty, time to move. He doubted if SPECTRE's surveillance team would expect anyone to make a move before the early hours. He had not let the others know that he had slipped the spare charts from *Prospero* inside his jacket before they left the boat that afternoon. Now he spread them out on the round glass table in the centre of his sitting room and began to study the course from Garrison Bight to Shark Island, making notes. When he was satisfied that he had all the compass bearings correct, and a very good idea of how he could guide a boat to within safe distance of the island, Bond began to dress for action.

He peeled off the T-shirt and wriggled into a light black cotton rollneck from his case. The jeans were replaced by a pair of black slacks, which he always packed. Next, he took out the wide belt which had been so useful when Der Haken had him locked up in Salzburg. He removed the Q Branch Toolkit and spread the contents out on the table. He checked the small explosive charges and their electronic connectors, adding from the false bottom of his second briefcase four small flat packets of plastique explosive, each no larger than a stick of chewing gum. Into the inner pockets of the belt he fitted four small lengths of fuse, some extra thin electric wire, half a dozen tiny detonators, a miniature pin-light torch, not much larger than the filter of a cigarette – and one other very important item.

Together the explosives would not dispose of an entire building, but they could be useful with locks or door hinges. He buckled on the belt, threading it through the loops on his trousers, then opened up the shoulder bag which contained the wet suit and snorkelling equipment. Sweating a little, he struggled into the wet suit and clipped the knife into place on the belt. The ASP, two spare magazines, the charts and the baton he put into the waterproof pouch threaded on to the belt. He carried the flippers, mask, underwater torch and snorkel in the shoulder bag.

Leaving the suite, he kept inside the hotel for as long as possible. There was still a great deal of noise coming from the bars, restaurant and makeshift dance floor and he finally emerged through an exit on the ocean side of the festivities.

Squatting down with his back against the wall, Bond unzipped the shoulder bag and pulled on the flippers, then slowly edged himself towards the water. The music and laughter were loud behind him as he climbed over the short stretch of rock marking the right-hand boundary of the hotel bathing area. He washed the mask out, slipped it on and adjusted the snorkel. Grasping the torch, he slid straight down into the water. He swam gently round the metal shark guard which protected swimmers using the hotel beach. It took about ten minutes to find the thick wooden piles under the Havana Docks bar deck, but he surfaced only a couple of metres from the moored motor boat.

Any sound he made clambering aboard would not have been heard above the noise coming from the hotel, and once inside the neat little craft, he could quickly check the fuel gauges with the pin-light torch. The beach staff were efficient and the tank had been filled, presumably ready for the next morning's work.

He cast off using his hands to manoeuvre the speed boat from under the pier. He then allowed it to drift, occasionally guiding it with the flat of his hand in the water, heading north, into the Gulf of Mexico, silently passing the Standard Oil pier.

The boat was about a kilometre and a half out when Bond switched on the riding lights. He moved aft to prime and start the motor. It fired at the first pull, and he had to scramble quickly forward and swing himself behind the wheel, one hand on the throttle. He opened up, glancing down at the small luminous dial on the compass, and silently thanked the Pier House for the care they took in keeping the boat in order.

Minutes later, he was cruising carefully along the coast, fumbling with the pouch to pull out the charts and take his first visual fix. He could not risk running the speed boat at anywhere approaching its full speed. The night was clear, and the moon was up, but Bond still had to peer into the dark water ahead. He spotted the exit point from Garrison Bight and began negotiating the tricky sandbars, cruising slowly, occasionally feeling the shallow draught of the boat touch the sand. Twenty minutes later he cleared the reef and set course for Shark Island.

Ten minutes passed, then another ten, before he caught a glimpse of lights. Soon afterwards he cut the engine and drifted in towards shore. The long dark slice of land stood out against the horizon, twinkling with lights from buildings set among trees. He leaned over, washed out his mask again, took up the torch, and, for the second time that night, dropped into the sea.

He remained on the surface for a while, judging that he was a couple of kilometres offshore. Then he heard the drumming of engines and saw a small craft rounding the island to his left, searching the waters with a powerful spotlight. Tamil Rahani's regular patrol, he thought. There would be at least two boats like this keeping a constant vigil. He took in air and dived, swimming steadily but conserving energy against any emergency.

He surfaced twice on the way in, to discover the second time that they had found the speed boat. The patrol craft had stopped and voices drifted over the water. He was less than a kilometre from shore and he was concerned now about the possibility of meeting sharks. The island would hardly be named after the creatures were they not known to haunt its vicinity.

Suddenly he came up against the heavy wire mesh of shark guard, around sixty metres from the beach. Clinging on to the strong metal, he could see lights shining brightly from picture windows in a large house. There were floodlights in the grounds. Looking back, he saw the spotlight from the patrol boat and heard its engine rise again. They were coming to look for him.

He heaved himself up on to the metal bar that topped the protective fence. One flipper caught awkwardly in the mesh, and he lost a few precious seconds disentangling himself before finally lowering his body into the water on the far side.

Again, he dived deep, swimming a little faster now that he was almost there. He had gone about ten metres when instinct warned him of danger: something was close by in the water. Then the bump jarred his ribs, throwing him to one side.

Bond turned his head and saw swimming beside him, as though keeping station with him, the ugly, wicked snout of a bull shark. The protective fence was not there to keep the creatures out but to make sure that an island guard of sharks remained close inshore – the favourite hunting ground of the dangerous bull shark.

The shark had bumped him but had not attempted to turn and attack, which meant that it was either well fed or had not yet sized up Bond as an enemy. He knew his only salvation was to remain calm, not to antagonise the shark, and certainly not knowingly to transmit fear – though he was probably doing that at the moment.

Still keeping pace with the shark, he slid his right hand down to the knife handle, his fingers closing around it, ready to use the weapon at a second's notice. He knew that on no account must he drop his legs. If he did that, the shark would recognise him immediately as prey, and the bull shark could move like a racing boat. The most dangerous moment lay ahead, and not very far ahead, when he reached the beach. There Bond would be at his most vulnerable.

As he felt the first touch of sand under his belly, he was aware of the shark dropping back. He swam on until his flippers began to churn sand. In that moment, he knew the shark was behind him, probably even beginning to build up speed for the strike.

Later Bond thought that he had seldom moved as quickly in water. He gave a last mighty push forward, bringing his feet down, then he raced for the beach, in an odd splayfooted, hopping run made necessary by the flippers. He reached the surf and rolled to the left just in time. The bull shark's snout, jaws wide and snapping, broke through the foaming water, missing him by inches.

Bond continued to roll, trying to propel himself forward, for he had heard of bull sharks coming right out of the water to attack. Two metres up the beach, he lay still, panting, feeling his stomach reel with a stab of fear.

Instantly his subconscious told him to move. He was on the island, and heaven alone knew with what other guardians SPECTRE had surrounded their headquarters. He kicked off the flippers and ran forward, crouching, to the first line of palms and undergrowth. There he squatted to take stock. First he had to dump the mask, snorkel and flippers. He pushed them under some bushes. The air was balmy and the sweet smell of night-blooming tropical flowers came to his nostrils.

He could detect no sounds of movement coming from the

grounds, which were well-lit and laid out with paths, small water gardens, trees, statues and flowers. A low murmur of voices came from the house. It was built like a pyramid lifted high above the ground on great polished steel girders. He could make out three storeys, each with a metal balcony running around the whole of the building. Some of the large picture windows were partly open, others had curtains drawn across them. On top of the building a forest of communications aerials stretched up like some avant-garde sculpture.

Gently, Bond reached into the waterproof pouch and drew out the ASP, slipping off the safety catch. He was breathing normally now, and using the trees and statues for cover he moved stealthily and silently towards the huge modern pyramid. As he got closer, he saw there were several ways into the place. A giant spiral staircase running up through the centre and three sets of metal steps, one on each side, which zig-zagged from one balcony to the next.

He crossed the last piece of open ground and stood to listen for a moment. The voices had ceased; he thought he could hear the patrol boat, far out to sea. Nothing else.

Bond began to climb the open zig-zagging stairs to the first level, his feet touching the fretted metal noiselessly, his body held to the left so that his right hand, clutching the ASP, was constantly ready. Standing on the first terrace, he waited, his head cocked. Just ahead of him there was a large sliding picture window, the curtains only partially drawn, and one section open. He crossed to the window and peered in.

The room was white, furnished with glass tables, soft white armchairs, and valuable modern paintings. A deep pile white carpet covered the floor. In the centre was a large bed, with electronic controls that could adjust any section to any angle, to improve the comfort of the patient who now lay in it.

Tamil Rahani was propped up with silk-covered pillows, his eyes closed, and his head turned to one side. Despite the shrunken face with skin the colour of parchment, Bond recognised him immediately. On their previous meetings, Rahani had been smooth, short and dapper, attractive in a military kind of way. Now the heir to the Blofeld fortune was reduced to this human doll, dwarfed by the seductive luxury of the high-tech bed.

Bond slid open the window, and stepped inside. Moving like a cat to the end of the bed, he gazed down on the man who controlled SPECTRE.

Now I can have him, he thought. Now, why not? Kill him now and you may not ruin SPECTRE, but at least you'll decapitate it – just as its leader wants you decapitated.

Taking a deep breath, Bond raised the ASP. He was only a few steps from Rahani's head. One squeeze of the trigger and it would be obliterated, and he could be away, hiding in the grounds until he found a way to get off the island.

As he began to squeeze the trigger, he thought he felt a small gust of air on the back of his head.

'I don't think so, James. We've brought you too far to let you do what God's going to do soon enough.' The voice came from behind him.

'Just drop the gun, James. Drop it, or you'll be dead before you can even move.'

He was stunned by the voice. The ASP fell with a noisy thump to the floor and Tamil Rahani stirred and groaned in his sleep.

'Okay, you can turn around now.'

Bond turned to look at Nannie Norrich, who stood in the window, an Uzi machine pistol held against her slim hip.

18

MADAME AWAITS

'I'm sorry it had to be like this, James. You lived up to your reputation. Every girl should have one.'

The grey eyes were as cold as the North Sea in December, and the words meant nothing.

'Not as sorry as I am.' Bond allowed himself a smile which neither the muzzle of the Uzi, nor Nannie Norrich deserved. 'You and Sukie, eh? You really did take me in. Is it private enterprise, or do you work for one of the organisations?'

'Not Sukie, James. Sukie's for real,' she replied flatly. Any feelings she might have had were well under control. 'She's in bed at the Pier House. I slipped her what the old gumshoe movies would call a Mickey Finn – a very strong one. We had coffee on room service after we left you. And I provided a service of my own. You'll be long gone by the time she wakes up. If she does wake up.'

Bond glanced at the bed. The shrunken figure of Tamil Rahani had not moved. Time. He needed time. Time for some fast talking, and a little luck. He tried to sound casual.

'Originally, a Mickey Finn was a laxative for horses. Did you know that?'

She took no notice. 'You look like a black Kermit the Frog in that gear, James. It doesn't suit you, so – very slowly – I want you to take it off.'

Bond shrugged. 'If you say so.'

'I do, and please don't be foolish. The tiniest move and I won't hesitate to take your legs off with this.' The muzzle of the Uzi moved a fraction.

Slowly, and with a certain amount of difficulty, Bond began to take off the wet suit. All the time, he tried to keep her talking, picking questions with care.

'You really did have me fooled, Nannie. After all, you saved me several times.'

'More than you know.' Her voice was level and emotionless. 'That was my job, or at least the job I said I'd try to do.'

'You wasted the German – what was his name? Conrad Tempel – on the road to Strasbourg?'

'Oh, yes, and there were a couple before that who had latched on to you. I dealt with them. On the boat to Ostend.'

Bond nodded, acknowledging that he knew about the men on the ferry. 'And Cordova – the Rat, the Poison Dwarf?'

'Guilty.'

'The Renault?'

'That took me a little by surprise. You helped a great deal, James. Quinn was a thorn in the flesh, but you helped again. I was simply your guardian angel. That was my job.'

He finally pulled off the wet suit, standing there in the black slacks and rollneck.

'What about Der Haken? The mad cop.'

Nannie gave a frosty smile. 'I had some help there. My own private panic button – Der Haken was briefed; he thought I was a go-between for himself and SPECTRE. When he had outlived his usefulness, Colonel Rahani sent in the heavy mob to dispose of him. They wanted to take you as well, but the Colonel let me carry on – though there was a penalty clause: my head was on the block if I lost you after that. And I nearly did, because I was responsible for the vampire bat. Lucky for you that Sukie came along to save you when she did. But that gave me a hard time with SPECTRE. They've been experimenting with the beasts here. It was meant to give you rabies. You were a sort of guinea pig, and the plan was to get you to Shark Island before the symptoms became apparent. The Colonel wants your head, but he wanted to see the effect of the rabies before they shortened you, as they say.'

She moved the Uzi again. 'Let's have you against the wall, James. The standard position, feet apart, arms stretched. We don't want to find you're carrying any nasty little toys, do we?'

She frisked him expertly, and then began to remove his belt. It was the action of a trained expert, and something Bond had dreaded. 'Dangerous things, belts,' she said, undoing the buckle, then unthreading it from the loops.'Oh, yes. This one especially. Very cunning.' She had obviously detected the Toolkit.

'If SPECTRE has someone like you on the payroll, Nannie, why bother with a charade like this competition – the Head Hunt?'

'I'm not,' she said curtly. 'Not on the payroll, I mean. I entered the competition as a freelance. I've done a little work for them before, so we came to an arrangement. They put me on a retainer, and I stood to get a percentage of the prize money if I won – which I have done. The Colonel has great faith in me. He saw it as a way of saving money.'

As though he had heard talk of himself, the figure on the bed stirred.

'Who is it? What . . . Who?'

The voice, so commanding and firm the last time Bond had heard it, was now as wasted as the body.

'It's me, Colonel Rahani,' said Nannie respectfully.

'The Norrich girl?'

'Nannie, yes. I've brought you a present.'

'Help . . . Sit up . . .' Rahani croaked.

'I can't at the moment. But I'll press the bell.'

Bond, leaning forward, hands spread against the wall, heard her move, but knew he had no chance of taking precipitate action. Nannie was fast and accurate at the best of times. Now, with her quarry cornered, her trigger finger would be very itchy.

'You can stand up now, James, slowly,' she said a couple of seconds later.

He pushed himself from the wall.

'Turn around – slowly – with your arms stretched out and feet apart, then lean back against the wall.'

Bond did as he was told, regaining a full view of the room just as the door to his right opened. Two men entered with guns in their hands.

'Relax,' Nannie said softly. 'I've brought him.'

They were the usual SPECTRE specimens, one fair-haired, the other balding; both big muscular men with wary eyes and cautious, quick movements.

The fair one smiled. 'Oh, good. Well done, Miss Norrich.' His English bore the trace of a Scandinavian accent. The bald one merely nodded.

They were followed by a short man, dressed casually in white shirt and trousers, his face distorted by the right corner of his mouth, which seemed permanently twisted towards the right ear.

'Dr McConnell,' Nannie greeted him.

'Aye, so it's you, Mistress Norrich. Ye've brought yon man the Colonel's always raving about, then?'

His face reminded Bond of a bizarre ventriloquist's dummy as he spoke in his exaggeratedly Scottish accent. A tall, masculine-looking nurse plodded in his wake, a big, raw-boned woman with flaxen hair.

'So, how's ma patient, then?' McConnell asked as he stood by the bed.

'I think he wants to see the present I've brought for him, Doctor.' Nannie's eyes never left Bond. Now she had him, she was taking no chances.

The doctor gave a signal to the nurse, who moved towards the white bedside table. She picked up a flat black control box the size of a man's wallet, attached to an electric cable that snaked under the bed. She pressed a button and the bedhead began to move upwards, raising Tamil Rahani into a sitting position. The mechanism made no more than a mild whirring noise.

'There. I said I'd do it, Colonel Rahani, and I did. Mr James

Bond, at your service.' The smallest hint of triumph could be detected in Nannie's voice.

There was a tired, wheezing cackle from Rahani as his eyes focused. 'An eye for an eye, Mr Bond. Apart from the fact that SPECTRE has wanted you dead for more years than either of us would care to recall, I have a personal score to settle with you.'

'Nice to see you in such a bad way,' Bond said with icy detachment.

'Ah! Yes, Bond,' Rahani croaked. 'On the last occasion we met, you caused me to jump for my life. I didn't know then that I was jumping to my death. The bad landing jarred my spine, and that started the incurable disease from which I am now dying. Since you've caused the downfall of previous leaders of SPECTRE and decimated the Blofeld family, I regard it as a duty, as well as a personal privilege, to see you wiped from the face of the earth – hence the little contest.' He was rapidly losing strength, each word tiring him. 'A contest which was a gamble with the odds in SPECTRE's favour, for we took on Miss Norrich, a tried and true operator.'

'And you manipulated other contestants,' Bond said grimly. 'The kidnapping, I mean. I trust . . .'

'Oh, the delightful Scottish lady, and the famous Miss Moneypenny. You trust?'

'I think that's enough talking, Colonel,' said Dr McConnell, moving closer to the bed.

'No . . . no . . .' Rahani said, scarcely above a whisper. 'I want to see him depart this life before I go.'

'Then ya will, Colonel.' The doctor bent over the bed. 'Ye'll have to rest a while first, though.'

Rahani tried to speak to Bond, 'You said you trust . . .'

'I trust both ladies are safe, and that, for once, SPECTRE will act honourably and see they are returned in exchange for my head.'

'They are both here. Safe. They will be freed the moment your head is severed from your body.'

Rahani seemed to shrink even smaller as his head sank back on to the pillows. For a second Bond relived the last time he had seen the man, over the Swiss lake – strong, tough, outclassed – yet leaping from an airship to escape Bond's victory.

The doctor looked around at the hoods. 'Is everything prepared? For the . . . er . . . the execution?' He did not even glance at Bond.

'We've been ready for a long time.' The fair man gave his toothy smile again. 'Everything's in order.'

The doctor nodded. 'The Colonel hasn't got long, I fear. A day, maybe two. I have to give him medication now, and he will sleep for about three hours. Can you do it then?'

'Whenever.' The balding man nodded, then gave Bond a hard look. He had stony eyes the colour of granite.

The doctor signalled to the nurse and she started to prepare an injection.

'Give the Colonel an hour, he'll no be disturbed by being moved then. In an hour ye can move the bed into . . . what d'ye call it? The execution chamber?'

'Good a name as any,' the fair-haired man said. 'You want us to take Bond up?' he asked Nannie.

'You touch him and you're dead. I know the way. Just give me the keys.'

'I have a request.' Bond felt the first pangs of fear, but his voice was steady, even commanding.

'Yes? What is it?' asked Nannie almost diffidently.

'I know it'll make little difference, but I'd like to be sure about May and Moneypenny.'

Nannie looked across at the two armed guards and the fair one nodded and said, 'They're in the other two cells. Next to the death cell. You can manage him by yourself? You're sure?'

'I got him here, didn't I? If he gives me any trouble I'll take his legs off. The doctor can patch him up for the headectomy.'

From the bed, where he was administering the injection, McConnell gave a throaty chuckle. 'I like it, Mistress Norrich – headectomy, I like it verra much.'

'Which is more than can be said for me.' Bond sounded very cool. At the back of his mind he was already doing some calculations. The mathematics of escape.

The doctor chuckled again. 'If ye want tae get a head, get a Nannie, eh?'

'Let's go.' Nannie came close to prodding Bond with the Uzi. 'Hands above the head, fingers linked, arms straight. Go for the door. Move.'

Bond walked through the door and into a curving passage with a deep pile carpet and walls of sky blue. The passage, he reckoned, ran around the entire storey, and was probably identical to others on the floors above. The great house on Shark Island, though externally constructed as a pyramid, seemed to have a circular core.

At intervals along the passage were alcoves in Norman style, each containing an *objet d'art* or painting. Bond recognised at least two Picabias, a Duchamp, a Dali and a Jackson Pollock. Fitting, he thought, that SPECTRE should invest in surrealist artists.

They came to elevator doors of brushed steel, curved to fit the shape of the passage. Nannie ordered him to lean back with his hands against the wall again, while she summoned the elevator. It arrived as soundlessly as the doors slid open. Everything appeared to have been constructed to ensure constant silence. She ushered him into the circular cage of the elevator. The doors closed and although he saw Nannie press the second floor button, Bond could hardly tell whether they were moving upwards or down. Seconds later the doors opened again, on to a very different kind of passage – bare, with walls which looked like plain brick, and a flagstone floor that absorbed the sound of every footstep. The curved passage was blocked off at either end.

'The detention area,' Nannie explained. 'You want to see the hostages? Okay, move left.'

She stopped him in front of a door that could have been part of a movie set, made of black metal, with a heavy lock and a tiny Judas squint. Nannie waved the Uzi.

From what he could see, the interior appeared to be a comfortable but somewhat spartan bedroom. May lay asleep on the bed,
her chest rising and falling and her face peaceful.

'I understand they've been kept under mild sedation,' Nannie
said with just a glimmer of compassion in her voice. 'They take
only a second or two to be wakened for meals.'

She ushered him on, to a similar room where he saw Moneypenny on a similar bed, relaxed and apparently sleeping, like May.

Bond drew back and nodded.

'I'll take you to your final resting place, then, James.'

Any compassion had disappeared. They went back the way
they had come, this time stopping before not a door but an
electronic dial pad set into the wall. Nannie again made him
take up a safe position against the wall as she punched out a
code on the numbered buttons. A section of wall slid back, and
Bond was ordered forward.

His stomach turned over as they entered a large, bare room
with a row of deep comfortable chairs, like exclusive theatre
seats, set along one wall. There was a clinical table and a hospital
Gurney trolley, but the centrepiece, lit from above by enormous
spots, was a very real guillotine.

It looked smaller than Bond had expected, but that was probably due to the French Revolution movies filming the instrument from a low angle, with the blade sliding down between
very high, grooved posts. This instrument stood barely two
metres high, making it look like a model of all the Hollywood
representations he had seen.

There was no doubt that it would do the job. Everything was
there, from the stocks for head and hands at the bottom, and an
oblong plastic box to catch them once dismembered, to the
slanting blade waiting at the top between the posts.

A vegetable – a large cabbage, he thought – had been jammed
into the hole for the head. Nannie stepped forward and touched
one of the upright posts. He did not even see the blade fall, it
came down so fast. The cabbage was sliced neatly in two and

there was a heavy thud as the blade settled. It was a macabre and unnerving little episode.

'In a couple of hours or so . . .' Nannie said brightly.

She allowed him to stand for a minute, to take in the scene. Then she pointed him towards a cell door at the far side of the chamber, similar to those in the passage. It was directly in line with the guillotine.

'They've done it quite well, really,' said Nannie, almost admiringly. 'The first thing you'll see when they bring you out will be Madame La Guillotine.' She gave a little laugh. 'And the last thing too. They'll do you proud, James. I understand that Fin is to do the honours, and he's been instructed to wear full evening dress. It'll be an elegant occasion.'

'How many have received invitations?'

'Well, I suppose there are only about thirty-five people on the whole island. The communications people and guards will be working. Ten, possibly thirteen if you count me, and should the Colonel want the hostages present, which is unlikely . . .'

She stopped abruptly, realising that she was giving away too much information. Quickly she regained her composure. It did not matter if he knew or not. In two hours the blade would come thudding down, separating Bond's head from his body in a fraction of a second.

'Into the cell,' she said quietly. 'Enough is enough.' As he passed through the door she called, 'I suppose I should ask if you have a last request.'

Bond turned and smiled. 'Oh, most certainly, Nannie, but you're in no condition to supply it.'

She shook her head. 'I'm afraid not, my dear James. You've had that already – and very pleasant it was. You might even be pleased to hear that Sukie was furious. She's absolutely crazy about you. I should have brought her along. She would have been glad to comply.'

'I was going to ask you about Sukie.'

'What about her?'

'Why haven't you killed her? You're a pro. You know the form. I would never have left someone like Sukie lying around, even in a drugged stupor. I'd have made sure she was silenced for good and all.'

'Maybe I have killed her. The dosage was near lethal.' Nannie's voice dropped, sounding slightly sad. 'But you're quite right, James. I should have made certain. There's no room for sentiment in our business. But . . . well, I suppose I held back. We've been very close, and I've always managed to hide my darker side from her. You need someone to like you, when you do these kind of things: you need to be loved, or don't you find that? You know, when I was at school with Sukie - before I discovered men – I was in love with her. She's been good to me. But you're right. When we've finished with you, I shall have to go back and finish her too.'

'How did you manage to engineer that meeting between Sukie and me?'

Nannie gave a tiny explosion of laughter. 'That really was an accident. I was playing it very much by ear. I knew where you were because I'd stuck a homer on your Bentley. I had it done on the boat. Sukie really did insist on making that part of the journey alone, and you *did* save her. I was going to set up something, depending where you were staying, because I knew you were heading towards Rome, as she was. It's funny, but the pair of you played right into my hands. Now, anything else?'

'Last requests?'

'Yes.'

Bond shrugged. 'I have simple tastes, Nannie. I also know when I'm beaten. I'll have a plate of scrambled eggs and a bottle of Taittinger – the '73, if that's possible.'

'In my experience, anything's possible with SPECTRE. I'll see what I can do.'

She was gone, the cell door slamming shut with a heavy thump. The cell was a small room, bare but for a metal bed covered with one blanket. Bond waited for a moment before going to the door. The flap over the Judas squint was closed, but he would have to be quick and careful. The silence of the place was against him; someone could be outside the door without his even knowing it.

Slowly, Bond undid the waistband of his slacks. Very rarely did he leave things to chance these days. Nannie had removed his belt and found Q Branch's Toolkit. The extra piece of equipment he had taken from his briefcase back at the Pier House had been the spare one he now needed. The black slacks were also made by Q Branch, and contained hidden compartments stitched into the waistband. They were well nigh undetectable. It took him just over a minute to remove the equipment from its secure hiding places. At least he knew there was a fair chance of his being able to release the cell door so that he could get as far as the execution chamber. After that, who knew?

He reckoned he had half an hour before they brought the food. In that time he must establish whether he could open the cell door. For the second time in a matter of days he went to work with the picklocks.

Unexpectedly, the cell lock was simple, a straightforward mortice that could be manipulated easily by two of the picks. He had it open and closed again in less than five minutes. Opening it the second time, he pushed at the cell door and walked out into the execution chamber. It was eerie, with the guillotine standing there in the centre of the room. He began a reconnaissance, and soon discovered he could find the main door only because he remembered roughly where it was located. It was operated electronically and fitted so well into the wall that it appeared to be part of it. If he placed the explosives correctly he might just do it, but the chances of finding the right position to blow the electronic locks would be more a matter of luck than judgment.

He returned to the cell, locked the door behind him and pushed the Toolkit out of sight under the blanket. He realised that the chances of blowing the execution chamber door were remote.

Bond racked his brains in an attempt to come to some resolution. He even considered destroying the guillotine itself. But he knew that this would be a hopeless act of folly, and a waste of good explosives. They would still have him, and there was more than one way of separating a man from his head.

The food was brought to him by Nannie herself, with the balding guard in attendance, the knuckles of his hands white as he grasped the Uzi.

'I said nothing was impossible for SPECTRE,' Nannie said without smiling as she indicated the Taittinger.

Bond simply nodded, and they left. As the cell door was closing, he felt he had been given one tiny morsel of hope. He heard the balding man mumble to Nannie,

'The old man's sleeping. We're going to bring him through now.'

Rahani was to be brought up in good time, so that he could wake from his medication already in position. As long as the nurse did not stay with him, Bond might just do it. The idea now formed in his mind as he ate the scrambled eggs and drank the champagne. He was glad he had asked for the '73. It was an excellent year.

He thought he could hear sounds from the other side of the door and he put his ear hard against the metal, straining to catch the slightest noise. Almost by intuition, he knew there was somebody approaching the door.

Quickly Bond stretched himself on the bed, still alert for any sound, until he was sure that he heard the Judas squint move back and then into place again. He counted off five minutes, then took out the Toolkit, leaving the explosives and detonators hidden for the time being. For the second time, he went to work on the lock. When the door swung open he found the chamber in darkness but for the glow of a bedside lamp, by which he could just see Tamil Rahani's electronically operated bed.

He crossed the chamber swiftly. Rahani lay silent and sleeping. Bond touched the control pad for the bed, discovered that its wire came from below the mattress, and followed it under the bed. What he saw gave him hope, and he crossed back to the cell to fetch the Toolkit, explosives and pin-light torch.

He slid quickly under the bed on his back, and in the darkness sought out the small electronic sensor box which moved the bedhead up and down to raise and lower Rahani. The cable ran to a switching box, bolted more or less centrally on to the underside of the bed. From it a power lead was laid to a mains plug in the wall. Wires ran from the switching box to the various sensors which adjusted each section to different angles. He was interested in the wires which connected the switching box to the bedhead sensor. Stretching forward cautiously, Bond turned off the power switch in the wall and then began to work on the slim bedhead sensor wires.

First he cut them and trimmed off about a centimetre of their plastic coating. Then he collected together every piece of plastic explosive he had managed to bring in. This he moulded to the edge of the sensor, finally inserting an electronic detonator, its two wires hanging loose and short from the plastique.

All that remained now was to plait together the wires as before, only this time adding a third wire to each pair – the wires from the detonator. In the Toolkit there was a minute roll of insulating tape no wider than a single book match. It took a little time, but he succeeded in insulating one set of wires from the others, thereby making sure that no bare wire could touch another by somebody moving the bed.

Finally, he gathered up all the contents of the Toolkit, turned on the mains power again and returned to the cell. He locked the door with the picks and once more hid the Toolkit.

The relatively small amount of explosives should be detonated the moment anyone pressed the control button to raise the bedhead. When – and he had to admit if – his device worked, he would have to move like lightning. Now he could only wait and hope.

It seemed like an eternity before he heard, quite suddenly, the key in the cell door. The fair-haired guard called Fin stood there in full evening dress and white gloves. Behind and to his right the balding man – also in tails – carried a heavy silver dish. They were going to do this in style, Bond thought. His head would be presented to the dying Tamil Rahani on a silver charger, in imitation of the old legends and myths.

Nannie Norrich appeared from behind the balding man and for the first time Bond saw her, under the glare of the lights, probably in her true persona. She wore a long dark dress, her hair loose and her face so heavily made up that it looked more like a tartish mask than the face of the charming woman he thought he had known. Her smile was a reflection of ugly perversity.

'Madame La Guillotine awaits you, James Bond,' she said.

He squared his shoulders and stepped into the chamber, quickly taking in the entire scene. The sliding doors were open, and he saw something he had missed before – a small shutter in the wall next to them, now open and revealing a dial pad identical to the one in the passage.

Two more big men had joined the party and were standing just inside the door, each with the familiar stony expression, one carrying a hand gun, the other an Uzi. Another pair, also with hand guns, were positioned near Rahani's bed, as were Dr McConnell and his nurse.

'She awaits you,' Nannie prompted, and Bond took a further step into the room. It hasn't worked, he thought. Then he heard Rahani's voice, weak and thin from the bed.

'See . . .' he whined, 'must see. Raise me up.' And again, stronger, 'Raise me up!'

Bond's eyes flickered round the group once more. The nurse reached for the control.

He saw as if in close-up her finger press the button that would raise the bedhead. Then hell and confusion exploded in the room.

19

DEATH AND DESTRUCTION

For a few seconds, Bond could not be certain that he had heard an explosion, though he was aware of a great blast of scorching air pushing him backwards. After the flash it was as though somebody had clapped cupped hands over his ears.

Time stood still. Everything took on a dreamlike quality, the scene apparently enacted in slow motion. In reality, events were moving at high speed and two thoughts were repeated over and over in Bond's mind – survive, and save May and Moneypenny.

He saw the remains of Rahani's bed blazing in the far corner to his right. There was nothing left of Rahani himself. Pieces of him had been spattered over the doctor, the nurse and the two guards who had been standing close to the explosion. He was aware of the doctor suddenly pitching forward into the fire where the centre of the bed had been. The nurse stood petrified, her head back, clothes ripped from her burned body. From her mouth came a drawn-out, strangled scream before she too fell towards the fire.

The two guards had been lifted up and hurled across the room, one towards the guillotine, the other with one arm half-severed and flapping, towards the man with the Uzi stationed by the door. He was knocked back against the door, his arm jerking forward so that the Uzi skated across the floor to land just in front of the guillotine, on the opposite side to Bond. The fourth guard appeared to be unhurt but dazed, his hand limp. He let go of his pistol and it slid, spinning towards Bond.

Bond had stepped back into the cell as the nurse reached for the control. In spite of the ringing in his ears, and the dazzle in his eyes, he had been shielded from the blast. Now, still unable to see or hear properly, he stepped out automatically from the cell and stood like a man mesmerised, staring at the pistol sliding towards him. Then he flung himself at the weapon and was on his belly, hand grasping at the pistol, rolling and firing as he rolled, first at the remaining guard near the door, then at Fin and the balding man. Two rounds apiece, in the approved service fashion.

He heard the shots as tiny pops in his ears and knew he had scored with each round. The guard by the door went spinning backwards. Fin's white evening shirt was suddenly patterned with blood. The balding man sat splay-legged on the floor clutching his stomach, a surprised look on his face.

Bond span round, looking for Nannie. She was making a dive for the Uzi on the far side of the guillotine. She took the shortest route, her body flat on the ground, arms reaching across the stocks. He saw her hands close on the weapon just as he flung himself towards the guillotine, his arm lifted, and struck the projecting lever.

Even through his deafness, Bond heard the appalling thud and the awful scream as the blade sliced through Nannie's arms. He was conscious of the spurting blood, the never-ending scream and the fact that the fire was now pouring out thick, dark smoke. He paused only to grab the Uzi and shake off the detached arms with their hands clamped around the weapon. It took two hard shakes to free them from the machine pistol. Then he was outside in the passageway, which was also rapidly filling with smoke.

Turning, Bond looked at the electronic locking pad set into the wall. It seemed to be a simple numerical device, but then he saw that the bottom row contained red buttons and was marked 'Time lock'. There was a small strip of printed instructions below them: *Press Time button. Press Close. When doors shut press number*

of hours required. Then press Time button again. Doors will remain
inoperable until period of time set has elapsed.

His fingers stabbed at the Time, then Close buttons. The doors
slid shut. He pressed Two . . . Four . . . Time. Everyone in the
execution chamber was either dead or dying anyway. Putting
the doors on a twenty-four hour time lock just might hold back
the fire. Now for the hostages.

As he ran for the cell containing May, alarm bells began to
ring. Bond could hear them well enough. Either the fire had set
them off, or someone still with strength left had activated them
from inside the death chamber.

He reached the door of the first cell, looking around wildly for
any sign of a key. There were no keys. Standing well to one side
Bond fired a burst from the Uzi, not at the metal lock but at the
topmost hinge and the area around it. Bullets whined and
ricocheted in the passage, but they also threw out great splinters
of wood and Bond saw the door sag as the top part of the frame
gave way. He turned the Uzi on to the lower hinge, gave it two
fast bursts and leaped to one side as the slab of metal detached
itself from the wall, hesitated, then fell heavily to one side.

May cowered back on her bed, eyes wide with fear, looking as
though she was trying to push her body through the wall.

'It's okay, May! It's me!' he yelled.

'Mr James! Oh, my God, Mr James!'

'Just hang on there,' Bond shouted at her, realising he was
raising his voice too high because of his temporary deafness.
'Hang on while I get Moneypenny. Don't come out into the passage until I tell you!'

'Mr James, how did . . .' She began, but he was away, up the
passage to the next cell door, where he repeated the process with
the Uzi. The passage appeared to be filling fast with smoke.

'It's okay, Moneypenny,' he shouted breathlessly. 'It's okay.
It's the white knight come to take you off on the pommel of his
saddle, or something like that.'

She looked grey with fear, and was shaking badly.

'James! Oh, James. I thought . . . they told me . . .'

She rushed to him and threw her arms around his neck. Bond had to disentangle himself firmly from his Chief's Personal Assistant. He almost dragged her into the passage and pointed her towards May's cell.

'I'll need your help with May, Penny. We've still got to get out of here. There's a fire blazing along the passage and unless I'm mistaken, quite a number of people who don't really want to see us leave. So for God's sake, don't panic. Just get May out of here as quickly as you can, then do as I tell you.'

As soon as he saw her respond, he ran through the thickening smoke towards the elevator doors. *Never use elevators in the event of fire.* How many times had he seen that warning in hotels? Yet now there was no alternative. Like it or not, there appeared to be no other way out of the passage.

He got to the curved steel doors and jabbed at the button. Perhaps others were making their escape from the floors above by the same method. Maybe the mechanism had already been damaged. He could now hear the roaring of fire along the passage, behind the doors of the execution chamber.

Reaching out, Bond touched the curved metal doors and found them distinctly warm. He waited, jabbing again at the button, then checked the Uzi and the automatic pistol. The automatic was a big Stetchkin with a twenty round magazine, and he had only loosed off six shots. He tucked the almost empty Uzi under his left arm, holding the Stetchkin in readiness.

Moneypenny came slowly along the passage supporting May, just as the elevator doors opened to reveal four men in dark combat jackets. Bond took in the surprised looks and the slight movement as one of them began to reach towards a holster at his hip.

His thumb flicked the Stetchkin from single shot to automatic, and he turned his hand sideways – for the Stetchkin has a habit of pulling violently upwards on automatic fire. If turned sideways it would neatly stitch bullets from left to right. Bond fired a controlled six rounds and the four men were littering the floor of the elevator. He held up a hand to stop Moneypenny bringing May any closer. Quickly he hauled the bodies out of the cage, jamming one of them across the doors to keep them from closing while he performed the task.

In less than thirty seconds he was ushering May and Moneypenny towards the lift. It was rapidly becoming very hot, and as soon as they were inside he pressed the Down button, keeping his finger on it for five or six seconds. When the doors next opened, they were facing the curved passage leading to Tamil Rahani's room.

'Slowly,' he warned May and Moneypeny, 'take care.'

A burst of machine gun fire rattled in the distance. It crossed Bond's mind that something odd was now going on. A fire was obviously blazing above them, yet they would be the only targets for any of SPECTRE's people left on the island. Why then was there shooting going on that was not directed at them?

The door to Rahani's room was open. There was a violent burst of fire from within. Slowly Bond edged into the doorway. Two men dressed in dark combat jackets, like those in the elevator, manned a heavy machine gun set up near the big picture windows. They were firing down into the gardens. Beyond them Bond could see helicopters, their lights blinking red and green, hovering over the island. A star shell burst high in the night sky, and three sharp cracks followed by splintering glass left him in no doubt that the house itself was coming under attack.

He hoped that the men out there were on the side of the angels as he stepped into the room and placed four bullets neatly into the necks of the two machine gunners.

'Stay in the passage! Stay down!' he shouted back to May and Moneypenny.

There was a moment's silence. Then Bond heard the unmistakable sound of boots clanking up the metal steps leading to the terrace balcony. Holding the pistol low, he called to those he could now see outside the window. 'Hold your fire! Escaping Hostages!'

A burly officer of the US Navy, brandishing a very large revolver, appeared at the window, followed by half a dozen armed naval ratings. Behind them he saw the white, frightened face of Sukie Tempesta, who cried out,

'It's them. It's Mr Bond and the people they were holding to ransom!'

'You Bond?' snapped the naval officer.

'Bond, yes. James Bond.' He nodded.

'Thank the Lord for that. Thought you were a gonner. Would have been but for this pretty little lady here. We've gotta move it, fast. This place will go up like a fired barn in no time.'

The leathery-faced man reached out, grasped Bond's wrist and propelled him towards the balcony, while three of his men hurried forward to help May and Moneypenny.

'Oh, James! James, it's so good to see you.' He had been thrown almost straight into the arms of the Principessa Sukie Tempesta and, for the second time in a matter of minutes, Bond found himself being kissed with an almost wild, skidding passion. This time he was in no hurry to break away.

Bond asked breathlessly what had happened as they were hustled through the gardens to the small pier. No sooner were they aboard than the coastguard cutter drew away, gathering speed. They looked back at the island. Other launches and cutters were circling, as were more helicopters, rattling their way around and keeping station with each other, some shining spotlights down into the beautifully laid out gardens.

'It's a long story, James,' Sukie said.

'Jesus!' said one of the coastguard officers through clenched teeth as the great pyramid that had been SPECTRE's headquarters spouted flame from the top of the structure, like an erupting volcano.

The helicopters had started to turn away, one making a low pass over the cutter. May and Moneypenny sat in the bows, being tended by a naval doctor. In the weird light from the Shark Island fire they both looked feverish and ill.

'She'll blow any minute,' the coastguard officer muttered and almost as he said it the building appeared to rise out of the island and hover for a second, surrounded by a sheet of dancing flame. Then it exploded in a flash of such dazzling intensity that Bond had to turn his head away.

When he looked again, the air seemed to be filled with burning fragments. A pall of smoke hung across the little hump that had been Shark Island.

He wondered if that was really the end of his old, old enemy, SPECTRE, or whether it would ever rise again, like some ungodly phoenix from the ashes of the death and destruction which he, James Bond, had caused.

20

CHEERS AND APPLAUSE

Sukie told her story once the cutter was inside the reef, and the sound of waves, wind and engines grew less, so that she did not have to shout.

'At first I couldn't believe my eyes – then, when Nannie made the telephone call, I knew,' she said.

'Just take it a step at a time.' Bond was still shouting as the ringing in his ears had not yet gone.

When Sukie and Nannie had left Bond the previous evening, Nannie had ordered coffee from room service.

'It arrived while I was in the bathroom touching up my face, so I told her to pour it,' Sukie told him.

She had left the door open, and in the mirror she saw Nannie put something in her cup from a bottle. 'I couldn't believe she was really up to no good, in fact I nearly taxed her about it. Thank goodness I didn't. I remember thinking she was trying to do me a good turn and keep me out of danger. I've always trusted her – she's been my closest friend since schooldays. I never suspected there was anything like . . . well . . . She was a very faithful friend you know, James. Right up until this.'

'Never trust a faithful friend,' Bond said with a wry smile. 'It always leads to tears before bedtime.'

Sukie had dumped the coffee and feigned sleep. 'She stood over me for a long time, lifted my eyelids and all that sort of thing. She used the telephone in the room. I don't know who she spoke to, but it was quite clear what she was up to. She said she was going to follow you. She thought you might try and make it to the island without us. "I've got him, though," she said. "Tell the Colonel I've got him."

'I stayed put for a while, in case Nannie came back – which she did, and made another call. Very fast. She said you'd taken the hotel motor boat and that she was following. She told them to keep a watch for you, but that you were her prisoner and she didn't want anyone else to take you. She kept saying she'd get you to the Colonel in one piece. He could divide you. Does that make sense?'

'Oh, a great deal of sense.'

Bond thought of the guillotine blade smashing down and removing Nannie Norrich's arms.

'Terrible,' he said, almost to himself. 'Really terrible. You know, I quite liked her – even grew fond of her.'

Sukie stared at him, but said nothing, as the cutter entered the small naval base harbour.

'And who's paying for all this luxury? That's what I want to know.' May was obviously well recovered.

'The Government,' said Bond, smiling at her. 'And if they don't, then I shall.'

'Well, it's a wicked waste of good money, keeping us all here in this verra expensive hotel. Ye ken how much it's costing here, Mr James?'

'I ken very well, May, and you're not to worry your head about it. We'll all be home soon enough, and this'll seem like a dream. Just enjoy it, and enjoy the sunset. You've never seen a Key West sunset, and it's truly one of God's miracles.'

'Och, I've seen sunsets in the Highlands, laddie. That's good enough for me.' Then she appeared to soften. 'It's guy kind of you though, Mr James, for getting me fit and well once more. I'll say that. But, oh, I'm longing for ma kitchen again, and looking after you.'

It was two days after what the local newspaper called 'The

Incident on Shark Island' and they had all been released as fit from the naval hospital that afternoon. Now May sat with Sukie and Bond on the deck in front of the Havana Docks bar at the Pier House Hotel. The sun was just starting its nightly show and the place was crowded. Again Sukie and Bond were eating the huge, succulent shrimps with little bowls of spicy sauce and drinking Calypso Daiquiris. May spurned both, making do with a glass of milk, about which she loudly expressed her hope that it was fresh.

'Lord, this really is the place where time stood still.' Sukie leaned over and kissed Bond lightly on the cheek. 'I went into a shop on Front Street this afternoon and met a girl who came here for two weeks. That was nine years ago.'

'I believe that is the effect it has on some people.' Bond gazed out to sea, thinking it was the last place he would want to stay for nine years. Too many memories were crowded in here – Nannie, the nice girl who had turned out to be a wanton and ruthless killer; Tamil Rahani, whom he had really met for the last time; SPECTRE, that dishonourable society willing even to cheat others of promised prizes for Bond's head.

'Penny for them?' Sukie asked.

'Just thinking that I wouldn't like to stay here for ever, but I wouldn't mind a week or two – perhaps to get to know you better.'

She smiled. 'I had the same thought. That's why I arranged for your things to be brought up to my suite, dear James.' The smile turned into a grin.

'You did what?' Bond's jaw dropped.

'You heard, darling. We've got a lot of time to make up.'

Bond gave her a long, warm look and watched the sky turn scarlet as the sun dropped behind the islands. Then he glanced towards the doors of the bar to see the ever-faithful Money-penny striding in their direction and beckoning to him.

He excused himself and went over to her. 'Signal from M,' she said, shooting dagger-like glances in Sukie's direction.

'Ah.' Bond waited.

' "Return soonest. Well done. M." ' Moneypenny intoned.

'You want to return home soonest?' he asked.

She nodded, a little sadly and said that she could understand why Bond might not wish to leave just yet.

'You could perhaps take May back,' he suggested.

'I booked the flight as soon as the signal came in. We leave tomorrow.' Efficient as ever.

'All of us?'

'No, James. I realised that I would never be able to thank you as I'd like to – for saving my life, I mean . . .'

'Oh, Penny, you mustn't . . .'

She put up a hand to silence him. 'No, James. I've booked a flight for May and myself. I've also sent a signal.'

'Yes?'

' "Returning immediately. 007 still requires remedial treatment that will take about three weeks." '

'Three weeks should do just nicely.'

'I thought so,' she said and turned, walking slowly back into the hotel.

'You actually had my stuff moved into your suite, you hussie?' Bond asked, once he had returned to Sukie.

'Everything you bought this afternoon – including the suitcase.'

Bond smiled. 'How can we? I mean, you're a Principessa – a Princess. It wouldn't be right.'

'Oh, we could call the book something like *The Princess and the Pauper*.' She grinned again – wickedly, with a dash of sensuality.

'I'm not a pauper, though,' said Bond, feigning huffiness.

'The prices here could fix that,' Sukie said, laughing, and at that moment the whole air and sky around them became crimson as sun took its dive for the day.

From Mallory Square, where crowds always watched the sunset, you could hear the cheers and applause.